Marriage à la mode

Marriage à la mode

by Mrs. Humphry Ward

Copyright © 1/29/2016
Jefferson Publication

ISBN-13: 978-1523772780

Printed in the United States of America

All rights reserved. No part of this book may be reprinted or reproduced or utilized in any form or by any electronic, mechanical, or other means, now known or hereafter invented, including photocopying and recording, or in any form of storage or retrieval system, without prior permission in writing from the publisher.'

Table of Contents

CHAPTER I 3
CHAPTER II 10
CHAPTER III 19
CHAPTER IV 25
    "He caught the hand, he gathered its owner into a pair of strong arms, and bending over her, he kissed her" 33
PART II 34
    THREE YEARS AFTER 34
CHAPTER V 34
CHAPTER VI 44
    "In the dead of night Daphne sat up in bed, looking at the face and head of her husband beside her on the pillow." 54
CHAPTER VII 55
CHAPTER VIII 63
    "Her whole being was seething with passionate and revengeful thought." 64
PART III 75
CHAPTER IX 75
CHAPTER X 84
CHAPTER XI 92
CHAPTER XII 99

CHAPTER I

"A stifling hot day!" General Hobson lifted his hat and mopped his forehead indignantly. "What on earth this place can be like in June I can't conceive! The tenth of April, and I'll be bound the thermometer's somewhere near eighty in the shade. You never find the English climate playing you these tricks."

Roger Barnes looked at his uncle with amusement.

"Don't you like heat, Uncle Archie? Ah, but I forgot, it's American heat."

"I like a climate you can depend on," said the General, quite conscious that he was talking absurdly, yet none the less determined to talk, by way of relief to some obscure annoyance. "Here we are sweltering in this abominable heat, and in New York last week they had a blizzard, and here, even, it was cold enough to give me rheumatism. The climate's always in extremes—like the people."

"I'm sorry to find you don't like the States, Uncle Archie."

The young man sat down beside his uncle. They were in the deck saloon of a steamer which had left Washington about an hour before for Mount Vernon. Through the open doorway to their left they saw a wide expanse of river, flowing between banks of spring green, and above it thunderous clouds, in a hot blue. The saloon, and the decks outside, held a great crowd of passengers, of whom the majority were women.

The tone in which Roger Barnes spoke was good-tempered, but quite perfunctory. Any shrewd observer would have seen that whether his uncle liked the States or not did not in truth matter to him a whit.

"And I consider all the arrangements for this trip most unsatisfactory," the General continued angrily. "The steamer's too small, the landing-place is too small, the crowd getting on board was something disgraceful. They'll have a shocking accident one of these days. And what on earth are all these women here for—in the middle of the day? It's not a holiday."

"I believe it's a teachers' excursion," said young Barnes absently, his eyes resting on the rows of young women in white blouses and spring hats who sat in close-packed chairs upon the deck—an eager, talkative host.

"H'm—Teachers!" The General's tone was still more pugnacious. "Going to learn more lies about us, I suppose, that they may teach them to school-children? I was turning over some of their school-books in a shop yesterday. Perfectly abominable! It's monstrous what they teach the children here about what they're pleased to call their War of Independence. All that we did was to ask them to pay something for their own protection. What did it matter to us whether they were mopped up by the Indians, or the French, or not? 'But if you want us to go to all the expense and trouble of protecting you, and putting down those fellows, why, hang it,' we said, 'you must pay some of the bill!' That was all English Ministers asked; and perfectly right too. And as for the men they make such a fuss about, Samuel Adams, and John Adams, and Franklin, and all the rest of the crew, I tell you, the stuff they teach American school-children about them is a poisoning of the wells! Franklin was a man of profligate life, whom I would never have admitted inside my doors! And as for the Adamses—intriguers—canting fellows!—both of them."

"Well, at least you'll give them George Washington." As he spoke, Barnes concealed a yawn, followed immediately afterwards by a look of greater alertness, caused by the discovery that a girl sitting not far from the doorway in the crowd outside was certainly pretty.

The red-faced, white-haired General paused a moment before replying, then broke out: "What George Washington might have been if he had held a straight course I am not prepared to say. As it is, I don't hesitate for a moment! George Washington was nothing more nor less than a rebel—a damned rebel! And what Englishmen mean by joining in the worship of him I've never been able to understand."

"I say, uncle, take care," said the young man, looking round him, and observing with some relief that they seemed to have the saloon to themselves. "These Yankees will stand most things, but——"

"You needn't trouble yourself, Roger," was the testy reply; "I am not in the habit of annoying my neighbours. Well now, look here, what I want to know is, what is the meaning of this absurd journey of yours?"

The young man's frown increased. He began to poke the floor with his stick. "I don't know why you call it absurd?"

"To me it seems both absurd and extravagant," said the other with emphasis. "The last thing I heard of you was that Burdon and Co. had offered you a place in their office, and that you were prepared to take it. When a man has lost his money and becomes dependent upon others, the sooner he gets to work the better."

Roger Barnes reddened under the onslaught, and the sulky expression of his handsome mouth became more pronounced. "I think my mother and I ought to be left to judge for ourselves," he said rather hotly. "We haven't asked anybody for money *yet*, Uncle Archie. Burdon and Co. can have me in September just as well as now; and my mother wished me to make some friends over here who might be useful to me."

"Useful to you. How?"

"I think that's my affair. In this country there are always openings—things turning up—chances—you can't get at home."

The General gave a disapproving laugh. "The only chance that'll help you, Roger, at present—excuse me if I speak frankly—is the chance of regular work. Your poor mother has nothing but her small fixed income, and you haven't a farthing to chuck away on what you call chances. Why, your passage by the *Lucania* alone must have cost a pretty penny. I'll bet my hat you came first class."

The young man was clearly on the brink of an explosion, but controlled himself with an effort. "I paid the winter rate; and mother who knows the Cunard people very well, got a reduction. I assure you, Uncle Archie, neither mother nor I is a fool, and we know quite well what we are about."

As he spoke he raised himself with energy, and looked his companion in the face.

The General, surveying him, was mollified, as usual, by nothing in the world but the youth's extraordinary good looks. Roger Barnes's good looks had been, indeed, from his childhood upward the distinguishing and remarkable feature about him. He had been a king among his schoolfellows largely because of them, and of the athletic prowess which went with them; and while at Oxford he had been cast for the part of Apollo in "The Eumenides," Nature having clearly designed him for it in spite of the lamentable deficiencies in his Greek scholarship, which gave his prompters and trainers so much trouble. Nose, chin, brow, the poising of the head on the shoulders, the large blue eyes, lidded and set with a Greek perfection, the delicacy of the lean, slightly hollow cheeks, combined with the astonishing beauty and strength of the head, crowned with ambrosial curls—these possessions, together with others, had so far made life an easy and triumphant business for their owner. The "others," let it be noted, however, had till now always been present; and, chief amongst them, great wealth and an important and popular father. The father was recently dead, as the black band on the young man's arm still testified, and the wealth had suddenly vanished, wholly and completely, in one of the financial calamities of the day. General Hobson, contemplating his nephew, and mollified, as we have said, by his splendid appearance, kept saying to himself: "He hasn't a farthing but what poor Laura allows him; he has the tastes of forty thousand a year; a very indifferent education; and what the deuce is he going to do?"

Aloud he said:

"Well, all I know is, I had a deplorable letter last mail from your poor mother."

The young man turned his head away, his cigarette still poised at his lips. "Yes, I know—mother's awfully down."

"Well, certainly your mother was never meant for a poor woman," said the General, with energy. "She takes it uncommonly hard."

Roger, with face still averted, showed no inclination to discuss his mother's character on these lines.

"However, she'll get along all right, if you do your duty by her," added the General, not without a certain severity.

"I mean to do it, sir." Barnes rose as he spoke. "I should think we're getting near Mount Vernon by this time. I'll go and look."

He made his way to the outer deck, the General following. The old soldier, as he moved through the crowd of chairs in the wake of his nephew, was well aware of the attention excited by the young man. The eyes of many damsels were upon him; and, while the girls looked and said nothing, their mothers laughed and whispered to each other as the young Apollo passed.

Standing at the side of the steamer, the uncle and nephew perceived that the river had widened to a still more stately breadth, and that, on the southern bank, a white building, high placed, had come into view. The excursionists crowded to look, expressing their admiration for the natural scene and their sense of its patriotic meaning in a frank, enthusiastic chatter, which presently enveloped the General, standing in a silent endurance like a rock among the waves.

"Isn't it fine to think of his coming back here to die, so simply, when he'd made a nation?" said a young girl—perhaps from Omaha—to her companion. "Wasn't it just lovely?"

Her voice, restrained, yet warm with feeling, annoyed General Hobson. He moved away, and as they hung over the taffrail he said, with suppressed venom to his companion: "Much good it did them to be 'made a nation'! Look at their press—look at their corruption—their divorce scandals!"

Barnes laughed, and threw his cigarette-end into the swift brown water.

"Upon my word, Uncle Archie, I can't play up to you. As far as I've gone, I like America and the Americans."

"Which means, I suppose, that your mother gave you some introductions to rich people in New York, and they entertained you?" said the General drily.

"Well, is there any crime in that? I met a lot of uncommonly nice people."

"And didn't particularly bless me when I wired to you to come here?"

The young man laughed again and paused a moment before replying.

"I'm always very glad to come and keep you company, Uncle Archie."

The old General reddened a little. Privately, he knew very well that his telegram summoning young Barnes from New York had been an act of tyranny—mild, elderly tyranny. He was not amusing himself in Washington, where he was paying a second visit after an absence of twenty years. His English soul was disturbed and affronted by a wholly new realization of the strength of America, by the giant forces of the young nation, as they are to be felt pulsing in the Federal City. He was up in arms for the Old World, wondering sorely and secretly what the New might do with her in the times to come, and foreseeing an ever-increasing deluge of unlovely things—ideals, principles, manners—flowing from this western civilization, under which his own gods were already half buried, and would soon be hidden beyond recovery. And in this despondency which possessed him, in spite of the attentions of Embassies, and luncheons at the White House, he had heard that Roger was in New York, and could not resist the temptation to send for him. After all, Roger was his heir. Unless the boy flagrantly misbehaved himself, he would inherit General Hobson's money and small estate in Northamptonshire. Before the death of Roger's father this prospective inheritance, indeed, had not counted for very much in the family calculations. The General had even felt a shyness in alluding to a matter so insignificant in comparison with the general scale on which the Barnes family lived. But since the death of Barnes *père*, and the complete pecuniary ruin revealed by that event, Roger's expectations from his uncle had assumed a new importance. The General was quite aware of it. A year before this date he would never have dreamed of summoning Roger to attend him at a moment's notice. That he had done so, and that Roger had obeyed him, showed how closely even the family relation may depend on pecuniary circumstance.

The steamer swung round to the landing-place under the hill of Mount Vernon. Again, in disembarkation, there was a crowd and rush which set the General's temper on edge. He emerged from it, hot and breathless, after haranguing the functionary at the gates on the inadequacy of the arrangements and the likelihood of an accident. Then he and Roger strode up the steep path, beside beds of blue periwinkles, and under old trees just bursting into leaf. A spring sunshine was in the air and on the grass, which had already donned its "livelier emerald." The air quivered with heat, and the blue dome of sky diffused it. Here and there a magnolia in full flower on the green slopes spread its splendour of white or pinkish blossom to the sun; the great river, shimmering and streaked with light, swept round the hill, and out into a pearly distance; and on the height the old pillared house with its flanking colonnades stood under the thinly green trees in a sharp light and shade which emphasized all its delightful qualities—made, as it were, the most of it, in response to the eagerness of the crowd now flowing round it.

Half-way up the hill Roger suddenly raised his hat.

"Who is it?" said the General, putting up his eyeglass.

"The girl we met last night and her brother."

"Captain Boyson? So it is. They seem to have a party with them."

The lady whom young Barnes had greeted moved toward the Englishmen, followed by her brother.

"I didn't know we were to meet to-day," she said gaily, with a mocking look at Roger. "I thought you said you were bored—and going back to New York."

Roger was relieved to see that his uncle, engaged in shaking hands with the American officer, had not heard this remark. Tact was certainly not Miss Boyson's strong point.

"I am sure I never said anything of the kind," he said, looking brazenly down upon her; "nothing in the least like it."

"Oh! oh!" the lady protested, with an extravagant archness. "Mrs. Phillips, this is Mr. Barnes. We were just talking of him, weren't we?"

An elderly lady, quietly dressed in gray silk, turned, bowed, and looked curiously at the Englishman.

"I hear you and Miss Boyson discovered some common friends last night."

"We did, indeed. Miss Boyson posted me up in a lot of the people I have been seeing in New York. I am most awfully obliged to her," said Barnes. His manner was easy and forthcoming, the manner of one accustomed to feel himself welcome and considered.

"I behaved like a walking 'Who's Who,' only I was much more interesting, and didn't tell half as many lies," said the girl, in a high penetrating voice. "Daphne, let me introduce you to Mr. Barnes. Mr. Barnes—Miss Floyd; Mr. Barnes—Mrs. Verrier."

Two ladies beyond Mrs. Phillips made vague inclinations, and young Barnes raised his hat. The whole party walked on up the hill. The General and Captain Boyson fell into a discussion of some military news of the morning. Roger Barnes was mostly occupied with Miss Boyson, who had a turn for monopoly; and he could only glance occasionally at the two ladies with Mrs. Phillips. But he was conscious that the whole group made a distinguished appearance. Among the hundreds of young women streaming over the lawn they were clearly marked out by their carriage and their clothes—especially their clothes—as belonging to the fastidious cosmopolitan class, between whom and the young school-teachers from the West, in their white cotton blouses, leathern belts, and neat short skirts, the links were few. Miss Floyd, indeed, was dressed with great simplicity. A white muslin dress, *à la* Romney, with a rose at the waist, and a black-and-white Romney hat deeply shading the face beneath—nothing could have been plainer; yet it was a simplicity not to be had for the asking, a calculated, a Parisian simplicity; while her companion,

Mrs. Verrier, was attired in what the fashion-papers would have called a "creation in mauve." And Roger knew quite enough about women's dress to be aware that it was a creation that meant dollars. She was a tall, dark-eyed, olive-skinned woman, thin almost to emaciation: and young Barnes noticed that, while Miss Floyd talked much, Mrs. Verrier answered little, and smiled less. She moved with a languid step, and looked absently about her. Roger could not make up his mind whether she was American or English.

In the house itself the crowd was almost unmanageable. The General's ire was roused afresh when he was warned off the front door by the polite official on guard, and made to mount a back stair in the midst of a panting multitude.

"I really cannot congratulate you on your management of these affairs," he said severely to Captain Boyson, as they stood at last, breathless and hustled, on the first-floor landing. "It is most improper, I may say dangerous, to admit such a number at once. And, as for seeing the house, it is simply impossible. I shall make my way down as soon as possible, and go for a walk."

Captain Boyson looked perplexed. General Hobson was a person of eminence; Washington had been very civil to him; and the American officer felt a kind of host's responsibility.

"Wait a moment; I'll try and find somebody." He disappeared, and the party maintained itself with difficulty in a corner of the landing against the pressure of a stream of damsels, who crowded to the open doors of the rooms, looked through the gratings which bar the entrance without obstructing the view, chattered, and moved on. General Hobson stood against the wall, a model of angry patience. Cecilia Boyson, glancing at him with a laughing eye, said in Roger's ear: "How sad it is that your uncle dislikes us so!"

"Us? What do you mean?"

"That he hates America so. Oh, don't say he doesn't, because I've watched him, at one, two, three parties. He thinks we're a horrid, noisy, vulgar people, with most unpleasant voices, and he thanks God for the Atlantic—and hopes he may never see us again."

"Well, of course, if you're so certain about it, there's no good in contradicting you. Did you say that lady's name was Floyd? Could I have seen her last week in New York?"

"Quite possible. Perhaps you heard something about her?"

"No," said Barnes, after thinking a moment. "I remember—somebody pointed her out at the opera."

His companion looked at him with a kind of hard amusement. Cecilia Boyson was only five-and-twenty, but there was already something in her that foretold the formidable old maid.

"Well, when people begin upon Daphne Floyd," she said, "they generally go through with it. Ah! here comes Alfred."

Captain Boyson, pushing his way through the throng, announced to his sister and General Hobson that he had found the curator in charge of the house, who sent a message by him to the effect that if only the party would wait till four o'clock, the official closing hour, he himself would have great pleasure in showing them the house when all the tourists of the day had taken their departure.

"Then," said Miss Floyd, smiling at the General, "let us go and sit in the garden, and feel ourselves aristocratic and superior."

The General's brow smoothed. Voice and smile were alike engaging. Their owner was not exactly pretty, but she had very large dark eyes, and a small glowing face, set in a profusion of hair. Her neck, the General thought, was the slenderest he had ever seen, and the slight round lines of her form spoke of youth in its first delicate maturity. He followed her obediently, and they were all soon in the garden again, and free of the crowd. Miss Floyd led the way across the grass with the General.

"Ah! now you will see the General will begin to like us," said Miss Boyson. "Daphne has got him in hand."

Her tone was slightly mocking. Barnes observed the two figures in front of them, and remarked that Miss Floyd had a "very—well—a very foreign look."

"Not English, you mean?—or American? Well, naturally. Her mother was a Spaniard—a South American—from Buenos Ayres. That's why she is so dark, and so graceful."

"I never saw a prettier dress," said Barnes, following the slight figure with his eyes. "It's so simple."

His companion laughed again. The manner of the laugh puzzled her companion, but, just as he was about to put a question, the General and the young lady paused in front, to let the rest of the party come up with them. Miss Floyd proposed a seat a little way down the slope, where they might wait the half-hour appointed.

That half-hour passed quickly for all concerned. In looking back upon it afterwards two of the party were conscious that it had all hung upon one person. Daphne Floyd sat beside the General, who paid her a half-reluctant, half-fascinated attention. Without any apparent effort on her part she became indeed the centre of the group who sat or lay on the grass. All faces were turned towards her, and presently all ears listened for her remarks. Her talk was young and vivacious, nothing more. But all she said came, as it were, steeped in personality, a personality so energetic, so charged with movement and with action that it arrested the spectators—not always agreeably. It was like the passage of a train through the darkness, when, for the moment, the quietest landscape turns to fire and force.

The comparison suggested itself to Captain Boyson as he lay watching her, only to be received with an inward mockery, half bitter, half amused. This girl was always awakening in him these violent or desperate images. Was it her fault that she possessed those brilliant eyes—eyes, as it seemed, of the typical, essential woman?—and that downy brunette skin, with the tinge in it of damask red?—and that instinctive art of lovely gesture in which her whole being seemed to express itself? Boyson, who was not only a rising soldier, but an excellent amateur artist, knew every line of the face by heart. He had drawn Miss Daphne from the life on several occasions; and from memory scores of times. He was not likely to draw her from life any more; and thereby hung a tale. As far as he was concerned the train had passed—in flame and fury—leaving an echoing silence behind it.

What folly! He turned resolutely to Mrs. Verrier, and tried to discuss with her an exhibition of French art recently opened in Washington. In vain. After a few sentences, the talk between them dropped, and both he and she were once more watching Miss Floyd, and joining in the conversation whenever she chose to draw them in.

As for Roger Barnes, he too was steadily subjugated—up to a certain point. He was not sure that he liked Miss Floyd, or her conversation. She was so much mistress of herself and of the company, that his masculine vanity occasionally rebelled. A little flirt!—that gave herself airs. It startled his English mind that at twenty—for she could be no more—a girl should so take the floor, and hold the stage. Sometimes he turned his back upon her—almost; and Cecilia Boyson held him. But, if there was too much of the "eternal womanly" in Miss Floyd, there was not enough in Cecilia Boyson. He began to discover also that she was too clever for him, and was in fact talking down to him. Some of the things that she said to him about New York and Washington puzzled him extremely. She was, he supposed, intellectual; but the intellectual women in England did not talk in the same way. He was equal to them, or flattered himself that he was; but Miss Boyson was beyond him. He was getting into great difficulties with her, when suddenly Miss Floyd addressed him:

"I am sure I saw you in New York, at the opera?"

She bent over to him as she spoke, and lowered her voice. Her look was merry, perhaps a little satirical. It put him on his guard.

"Yes, I was there. You were pointed out to me."

"You were with some old friends of mine. I suppose they gave you an account of me?"

"They were beginning it; but then Melba began to sing, and some horrid people in the next box said 'Hush!'"

She studied him in a laughing silence a moment, her chin on her hand, then said:

"That is the worst of the opera; it stops so much interesting conversation."

"You don't care for the music?"

"Oh, I am a musician!" she said quickly. "I teach it. But I am like the mad King of Bavaria—I want an opera-house to myself."

"You teach it?" he said, in amazement.

She nodded, smiling. At that moment a bell rang. Captain Boyson rose.

"That's the signal for closing. I think we ought to be moving up."

They strolled slowly towards the house, watching the stream of excursionists pour out of the house and gardens, and wind down the hill; sounds of talk and laughter filled the air, and the western sun touched the spring hats and dresses.

"The holidays end to-morrow," said Daphne Floyd demurely, as she walked beside young Barnes. And she looked smiling at the crowd of young women, as though claiming solidarity with them.

A teacher? A teacher of music?—with that self-confidence—that air as though the world belonged to her! The young man was greatly mystified. But he reminded himself that he was in a democratic country where all men—and especially all women—are equal. Not that the young women now streaming to the steamboat were Miss Floyd's equals. The notion was absurd. All that appeared to be true was that Miss Floyd, in any circumstances, would be, and was, the equal of anybody.

"How charming your friend is!" he said presently to Cecilia Boyson, as they lingered on the veranda, waiting for the curator, in a scene now deserted. "She tells me she is a teacher of music."

Cecilia Boyson looked at him in amazement, and made him repeat his remark. As he did so, his uncle called him, and he turned away. Miss Boyson leant against one of the pillars of the veranda, shaking with suppressed laughter.

But at that moment the curator, a gentle, gray-haired man, appeared, shaking hands with the General, and bowing to the ladies. He gave them a little discourse on the house and its history, as they stood on the veranda; and private conversation was no longer possible.

CHAPTER II

A sudden hush had fallen upon Mount Vernon. From the river below came the distant sounds of the steamer, which, with its crowds safe on board, was now putting off for Washington. But the lawns and paths of the house, and the formal garden behind it, and all its simple rooms upstairs and down, were now given back to the spring and silence, save for this last party of sightseers. The curator, after his preliminary lecture on the veranda, took them within; the railings across the doors were removed; they wandered in and out as they pleased.

Perhaps, however, there were only two persons among the six now following the curator to whom the famous place meant anything more than a means of idling away a warm afternoon. General Hobson carried his white head proudly through it, saying little or nothing. It was the house of a man who had wrenched half a continent from Great Britain; the English Tory had no intention whatever of bowing the knee. On the other hand, it was the house of a soldier and a gentleman, representing old English traditions, tastes, and manners. No modern blatancy, no Yankee smartness anywhere. Simplicity and moderate wealth, combined with culture—witness the books of the library—with landowning, a family coach, and church on Sundays: these things the Englishman understood. Only the slaves, in the picture of Mount Vernon's past, were strange to him.

They stood at length in the death-chamber, with its low white bed, and its balcony overlooking the river.

"This, ladies, is the room in which General Washington died," said the curator, patiently repeating the familiar sentence. "It is, of course, on that account sacred to every true American."

He bowed his head instinctively as he spoke. The General looked round him in silence. His eye was caught by the old hearth, and by the iron plate at the back of it, bearing the letters G. W. and some scroll work. There flashed into his mind a vision of the December evening on which Washington passed away, the flames flickering in the chimney, the winds breathing round the house and over the snow-bound landscape outside, the dying man in that white bed, and around him, hovering invisibly, the generations of the future.

"He was a traitor to his king and country!" he repeated to himself, firmly. Then as his patriotic mind was not disturbed by a sense of humour, he added the simple reflection—"But it is, of course, natural that Americans should consider him a great man."

The French window beside the bed was thrown open, and these privileged guests were invited to step on to the balcony. Daphne Floyd was handed out by young Barnes. They hung over the white balustrade together. An evening light was on the noble breadth of river; its surface of blue and gold gleamed through the boughs of the trees which girdled the house; blossoms of wild cherry, of dogwood, and magnolia sparkled amid the coverts of young green.

Roger Barnes remarked, with sincerity, as he looked about him, that it was a very pretty place, and he was glad he had not missed it. Miss Floyd made an absent reply, being in fact occupied in studying the speaker. It was, so to speak, the first time she had really observed him; and, as they paused on the balcony together, she was suddenly possessed by the same impression as that which had mollified the General's scolding on board the steamer. He was indeed handsome, the young Englishman!—a magnificent figure of a man, in height and breadth and general proportions; and in addition, as it seemed to her, possessed of an absurd and superfluous beauty of feature. What does a man want with such good looks? This was perhaps the girl's first instinctive feeling. She was, indeed, a little dazzled by her new companion, now that she began to realize him. As compared with the average man in Washington or New York, here was an exception—an Apollo!—for she too thought of the Sun-god. Miss Floyd could not remember that she had ever had to do with an Apollo before; young Barnes, therefore, was so far an event, a sensation. In the opera-house she had been vaguely struck by a handsome face. But here, in the freedom of outdoor dress and movement, he seemed to her a physical king of men; and, at the same time, his easy manner—which, however, was neither conceited nor ill-bred—showed him conscious of his advantages.

As they chatted on the balcony she put him through his paces a little. He had been, it seemed, at Eton and Oxford; and she supposed that he belonged to the rich English world. His mother was a Lady Barnes; his father, she gathered, was dead; and he was travelling, no doubt, in the lordly English way, to get a little knowledge of the barbarians outside, before he settled down to his own kingdom, and the ways thereof. She envisaged a big Georgian house in a spreading park, like scores that she had seen in the course of motoring through England the year before.

Meanwhile, the dear young man was evidently trying to talk to her, without too much reference to the gilt gingerbread of this world. He did not wish that she should feel herself carried into regions where she was not at home, so that his conversation ran amicably on music. Had she learned it abroad? He had a cousin who had been trained at Leipsic; wasn't teaching it trying sometimes—when people had no ear? Delicious! She kept it up, talking with smiles of "my pupils" and "my class," while they wandered after the others upstairs to the dark low-roofed room above the death-chamber, where Martha Washington spent the last years of her life, in order that from the high dormer window she might command the tomb on the slope below, where her dead husband lay. The curator told the well-known story. Mrs. Verrier, standing beside him, asked some questions, showed indeed some animation.

"She shut herself up here? She lived in this garret? That she might always see the tomb? That is really true?"

Barnes, who did not remember to have heard her speak before, turned at the sound of her voice, and looked at her curiously. She wore an expression—bitter or incredulous—which, somehow, amused him. As they descended again to the garden he communicated his amusement—discreetly—to Miss Floyd.

Did Mrs. Verrier imply that no one who was not a fool could show her grief as Mrs. Washington did? That it was, in fact, a sign of being a fool to regret your husband?

"Did she say that?" asked Miss Floyd quickly.

"Not like that, of course, but——"

They had now reached the open air again, and found themselves crossing the front court to the kitchen-garden. Daphne Floyd did not wait till Roger should finish his sentence. She turned on him a face which was grave if not reproachful.

"I suppose you know Mrs. Verrier's story?"

"Why, I never saw her before! I hope I haven't said anything I oughtn't to have said?"

"Everybody knows it here," said Daphne slowly. "Mrs. Verrier married three years ago. She married a Jew—a New Yorker—who had changed his name. You know Jews are not in what we call 'society' over here? But Madeleine thought she could do it; she was in love with him, and she meant to be able to do without society. But she couldn't do without society; and presently she began to dine out, and go to parties by herself—he urged her to. Then, after a bit, people didn't ask her as much as before; she wasn't happy; and her people began to talk to him about a divorce—naturally they had been against her marrying him all along. He said—as they and she pleased. Then, one night about a year ago, he took the train to Niagara—of course it was a very commonplace thing to do—and two days afterwards he was found, thrown up by the whirlpool; you know, where all the suicides are found!"

Barnes stopped short in front of his companion, his face flushing.

"What a horrible story!" he said, with emphasis.

Miss Floyd nodded.

"Yes, poor Madeleine has never got over it."

The young man still stood riveted.

"Of course Mrs. Verrier herself had nothing to do with the talk about divorce?"

Something in his tone roused a combative instinct in his companion. She, too, coloured, and drew herself up.

"Why shouldn't she? She was miserable. The marriage had been a great mistake."

"And you allow divorce for that?" said the man, wondering. "Oh, of course I know every State is different, and some States are worse than others. But, somehow, I never came across a case like that—first hand—before."

He walked on slowly beside his companion, who held herself a little stiffly.

"I don't know why you should talk in that way," she said at last, breaking out in a kind of resentment, "as though all our American views are wrong! Each nation arranges these things for itself. You have the laws that suit you; you must allow us those that suit us."

Barnes paused again, his face expressing a still more complete astonishment.

"You say that?" he said. "You!"

"And why not?"

"But—but you are so young!" he said, evidently finding a difficulty in putting his impressions. "I beg your pardon—I ought not to talk about it at all. But it was so odd that——"

"That I knew anything about Mrs. Verrier's affairs?" said Miss Floyd, with a rather uncomfortable laugh. "Well, you see, American girls are not like English ones. We don't pretend not to know what everybody knows."

"Of course," said Roger hurriedly; "but you wouldn't think it a fair and square thing to do?"

"Think what?"

"Why, to marry a man, and then talk of divorcing him because people didn't invite you to their parties."

"She was very unhappy," said Daphne stubbornly.

"Well, by Jove!" cried the young man, "she doesn't look very happy now!"

"No," Miss Floyd admitted. "No. There are many people who think she'll never get over it."

"Well, I give it up." The Apollo shrugged his handsome shoulders. "You say it was she who proposed to divorce him?—yet when the wretched man removes himself, then she breaks her heart!"

"Naturally she didn't mean him to do it in that way," said the girl, with impatience. "Of course you misunderstood me entirely!—*entirely!*" she added with an emphasis which suited with her heightened colour and evidently ruffled feelings.

Young Barnes looked at her with embarrassment. What a queer, hot-tempered girl! Yet there was something in her which attracted him. She was graceful even in her impatience. Her slender neck, and the dark head upon it, her little figure in the white muslin, her dainty arms and hands—these points in her delighted an honest eye, quite accustomed to appraise the charms of women. But, by George! she took herself seriously, this little music-teacher. The air of wilful command about her, the sharpness with which she had just rebuked him, amazed and challenged him.

"I am very sorry if I misunderstood you," he said, a little on his dignity; "but I thought you——"

"You thought I sympathized with Mrs. Verrier? So I do; though of course I am awfully sorry that such a dreadful thing happened. But you'll find, Mr. Barnes, that American girls——" The colour rushed into her small olive cheeks. "Well, we know all about the old ideas, and we know also too well that there's only one life, and we don't mean to have that one spoilt. The old notions of marriage—your English notions," cried the girl facing him—"make it tyranny! Why should people stay together when they see it's a mistake? We say everybody shall have their chance. And not one chance only, but more than one. People find out in marriage what they couldn't find out before, and so——"

"You let them chuck it just when they're tired of it?" laughed Barnes. "And what about the——"

"The children?" said Miss Floyd calmly. "Well, of course, that has to be very carefully considered. But how can it do children any good to live in an unhappy home?"

"Had Mrs. Verrier any children?"

"Yes, one little girl."

"I suppose she meant to keep her?"

"Why, of course."

"And the father didn't care?"

"Well, I believe he did," said Daphne unwillingly. "Yes, that was very sad. He was quite devoted to her."

"And you think that's all right?" Barnes looked at his companion, smiling.

"Well, of course, it was a pity," she said, with fresh impatience; "I admit it was a pity. But then, why did she ever marry him? That was the horrible mistake."

"I suppose she thought she liked him."

"Oh, it was he who was so desperately in love with her. He plagued her into doing it."

"Poor devil!" said Barnes heartily. "All right, we're coming."

The last words were addressed to General Hobson, waving to them from the kitchen-garden. They hurried on to join the curator, who took the party for a stroll round some of the fields over which George Washington, in his early married life, was accustomed to ride in summer and winter dawns, inspecting his negroes, his plantation, and his barns. The grass in these Southern fields was already high; there were shining fruit-trees, blossom-laden, in an orchard copse; and the white dogwood glittered in the woods.

For two people to whom the traditions of the place were dear, this quiet walk through Washington's land had a charm far beyond that of the reconstructed interior of the house. Here were things unaltered and unalterable, boundaries, tracks, woods, haunted still by the figure of the young master and bridegroom who brought Patsy Curtis there in 1759. To the gray-haired curator every foot of them was sacred and familiar; he knew these fields and the records of them better than any detail of his own personal affairs; for years now he had lived in spirit with Washington, through all the hours of the Mount Vernon day; his life was ruled by one great ghost, so that everything actual was comparatively dim. Boyson too, a fine soldier and a fine intelligence, had a mind stored with Washingtoniana. Every now and then he and the curator fell back on each other's company. They knew well that the others were not worthy of their opportunity; although General Hobson, seeing that most of the memories touched belonged to a period before the Revolution, obeyed the dictates of politeness, and made amends for his taciturnity indoors by a talkative vein outside.

Captain Boyson was not, however, wholly occupied with history or reminiscence. He perceived very plainly before the walk was over that the General's good-looking nephew and Miss Daphne Floyd were interested in each other's conversation. When they joined the party in the garden it seemed to him that they had been disputing. Miss Daphne was flushed and a little snappish when spoken to; and the young man looked embarrassed. But presently he saw that they gravitated to each other, and that, whatever chance combination might be formed during the walk, it always ended for a time in the flight ahead of the two figures, the girl in the rose-coloured sash and the tall handsome youth. Towards the end of the walk they became separated from the rest of the party, and only arrived at the little station just in time before the cars started. On this occasion again, they had been clearly arguing and disagreeing; and Daphne had the air of a ruffled bird, her dark eyes glittering, her mouth set in the obstinate lines that Boyson knew by heart. But again they sat together in the car, and talked and sparred all the way home; while Mrs. Verrier, in a corner of the carriage, shut her hollow eyes, and laid her thin hands one over the other, and in her purple draperies made a picture *à la Mèlisande* which was not lost upon her companions. Boyson's mind registered a good many grim or terse comments, as occasionally he found himself watching this lady. Scarcely a year since that hideous business at Niagara, and here she was in that extravagant dress! He wished his sister would not make a friend of her, and that Daphne Floyd saw less of her. Miss Daphne had quite enough bees in her own bonnet without adopting Mrs. Verrier's.

Meanwhile, it was the General who, on the return journey, was made to serve Miss Boyson's gift for monopoly. She took possession of him in a business-like way, inquiring into his engagements in Washington, his particular friends, his opinion of the place and the people, with a light-handed acuteness which was more than a match for the Englishman's instincts of defence. The General did not mean to give himself away; he intended, indeed, precisely the contrary; but, after every round of conversation Miss Boyson felt herself more and more richly provided with materials for satire at the expense of England and the English tourist, his invincible conceit, insularity, and condescension. She was a clever though tiresome woman; and expressed herself best in letters. She promised herself to write a "character" of General Hobson in her next letter to an intimate friend, which should be a masterpiece. Then, having led him successfully through the *rôle* of the comic Englishman abroad, she repaid him with information. She told him, not without some secret amusement at the reprobation it excited, the tragic story of Mrs. Verrier. She gave him a full history of her brother's honourable and brilliant career; and here let it be said that the *précieuse* in her gave way to the sister, and that she talked with feeling. And finally she asked him with a smile whether he admired Miss Floyd. The General, who had in fact been observing Miss Floyd and his nephew with some little uneasiness during the preceding half-hour, replied guardedly that Miss Floyd was pretty and picturesque, and apparently a great talker. Was she a native of Washington?

"You never heard of Miss Floyd?—of Daphne Floyd? No? Ah, well!"—and she laughed—"I suppose I ought to take it as a compliment, of a kind. There are so many rich people now in this queer country of ours that even Daphne Floyds don't matter."

"Is Miss Floyd so tremendously rich?"

General Hobson turned a quickened countenance upon her, expressing no more than the interest felt by the ordinary man in all societies—more strongly, perhaps, at the present day than ever before—in the mere fact of money. But Miss Boyson gave it at once a personal meaning, and set herself to play on what she scornfully supposed to be the cupidity of the Englishman. She produced, indeed, a full and particular account of Daphne Floyd's parentage, possessions, and prospects, during which the General's countenance represented him with great fidelity. A trace of recalcitrance at the beginning—for it was his opinion that Miss Boyson, like most American women, talked decidedly too much—gave way to close attention, then to astonishment, and finally to a very animated observation of Miss Floyd's slender person as she sat a yard or two from him on the other side of the car, laughing, frowning, or chattering with Roger.

"And that poor child has the management of it all?" he said at last, in a tone which did him credit. He himself had lost an only daughter at twenty-one, and he held old-fashioned views as to the helplessness of women.

But Cecilia Boyson again misunderstood him.

"Oh, yes!" she said, with a cool smile. "Everything is in her own hands—everything! Mrs. Phillips would not dare to interfere. Daphne always has her own way."

The General said no more. Cecilia Boyson looked out of the window at the darkening landscape, thinking with malice of Daphne's dealings with the male sex. It had been a Sleeping Beauty story so far. Treasure for the winning—a thorn hedge—and slain lovers! The handsome Englishman would try it next, no doubt. All young Englishmen, according to her, were on the look-out for American heiresses. Music teacher indeed! She would have given a good deal to hear the conversation of the uncle and nephew when the party broke up.

The General and young Barnes made their farewells at the railway station, and took their way on foot to their hotel. Washington was steeped in sunset. The White House, as they passed it, glowed amid its quiet trees. Lafayette Square, with its fountains and statues, its white and pink magnolias, its strolling, chatting crowd, the fronts of the houses, the long vistas of tree-lined avenues, the street cars, the houses, the motors, all the openings and distances of the beautiful, leisurely place—they saw them rosily transfigured under a departing sun, which throughout the day had been weaving the quick spells of a southern spring.

"Jolly weather!" said Roger, looking about him. "And a very nice afternoon. How long are you staying here, Uncle Archie?"

"I ought to be off at the end of the week; and of course you want to get back to New York? I say, you seemed to be getting on with that young lady?"

The General turned a rather troubled eye upon his companion.

"She wasn't bad fun," said the young man graciously; "but rather an odd little thing! We quarrelled about every conceivable subject. And it's queer how much that kind of girl seems to go about in America. She goes everywhere and knows everything. I wonder how she manages it."

"What kind of girl do you suppose she is?" asked the General, stopping suddenly in the middle of Lafayette Square.

"She told me she taught singing," said Roger, in a puzzled voice, "to a class of girls in New York."

The General laughed.

"She seems to have made a fool of you, my dear boy. She is one of the great heiresses of America."

Roger's face expressed a proper astonishment.

"Oh! that's it, is it? I thought once or twice there was something fishy—she was trying it on. Who told you?"

The General retailed his information. Miss Daphne Floyd was the orphan daughter of an enormously rich and now deceased lumber-king, of the State of Illinois. He had made vast sums by lumbering, and then invested in real estate in Chicago and Buffalo, not to speak of a railway or two, and had finally left his daughter and only child in possession of a fortune generally estimated at more than a million sterling. The money was now entirely in the girl's power. Her trustees had been sent about their business, though Miss Floyd was pleased occasionally to consult them. Mrs. Phillips, her chaperon, had not much influence with her; and it was supposed that Mrs. Verrier advised her more than anyone else.

"Good heavens!" was all that young Barnes could find to say when the story was told. He walked on absently, flourishing his stick, his face working under the stress of amused meditation. At last he brought out:

"You know, Uncle Archie, if you'd heard some of the things Miss Floyd was saying to me, your hair would have stood on end."

The General raised his shoulders.

"I dare say. I'm too old-fashioned for America. The sooner I clear out the better. Their newspapers make me sick; I hate the hotels—I hate the cooking; and there isn't a nation in Europe I don't feel myself more at home with."

Roger laughed his clear, good-tempered laugh. "Oh! I don't feel that way at all. I get on with them capitally. They're a magnificent people. And, as to Miss Floyd, I didn't mean anything bad, of course. Only the ideas some of the girls here have, and the way they discuss them—well, it beats me!"

"What sort of ideas?"

Roger's handsome brow puckered in the effort to explain. "They don't think anything's *settled*, you know, as we do at home. Miss Floyd doesn't. They think *they've* got to settle a lot of things that English girls don't trouble about, because they're just told to do 'em, or not to do 'em, by the people that look after them!"

"'Everything hatched over again, and hatched different,'" said the General, who was an admirer of George Eliot; "that's what they'd like, eh? Pooh! That's when they're young. They quiet down, like all the rest of the world."

Barnes shook his head. "But they *are* hatching it over again. You meet people here in society you couldn't meet at home. And it's all right. The law backs them up."

"You're talking about divorce!" said the General. "Aye! it's astounding! The tales one hears in the smoking-room after dinner! In Wyoming, apparently, six months' residence, and there you are. You prove a little cruelty, the husband makes everything perfectly easy, you say a civil good-bye, and the thing's done. Well, they'll pay for it, my dear Roger—they'll pay for it. Nobody ever yet trifled with the marriage law with impunity."

The energy of the old man's bearing became him.

Through Roger's mind the thought flashed: "Poor dear Uncle Archie! If he'd been a New Yorker he'd never have put up with Aunt Lavinia for thirty years!"

They turned into their hotel, and ordered dinner in an hour's time. Roger found some English letters waiting for him, and carried them off to his room. He opened his mother's first. Lady Barnes wrote a large and straggling hand, which required many sheets and much postage. It might have been observed that her son looked at the sheets for a minute, with a certain distaste, before he began upon them. Yet he was deeply attached to his mother, and it was from her letters week by week that he took his marching orders. If she only wouldn't ride her ideas quite so hard; if she would sometimes leave him alone to act for himself!

Here it was again—the old story:

"Don't suppose I put these things before you on *my* account. No, indeed; what does it matter what happens to me? It is when I think that you may have to spend your whole life as a clerk in a bank, unless you rouse yourself now (for you know, my dear Roger, though you have very good wits, you're not as frightfully clever as people have to be nowadays)—that I begin to despair. But that is *entirely* in your own hands. You have what is far more valuable than cleverness—you have a delightful disposition, and you are one of the handsomest of men. There! of course, I know you wouldn't let me say it to you in your presence; but it's true all the same. Any girl should be proud to marry you. There are plenty of rich girls in America; and if you play your cards properly you will make her and yourself happy. The grammar of that is not quite right, but you understand me. Find a nice girl—of course a *nice* girl—with a fortune large enough to put you back in your proper sphere; and it doesn't matter about me. You will pay my rent, I dare say, and help me through when I want it; but that's nothing. The point is, that I cannot submit to your career being spoiled through your poor father's mad imprudence. You must retrieve yourself—you *must*. Nobody is anything nowadays in the world without money; you know that as well as I do. And besides, there is another reason. You have got to forget the affair of last spring, to put it entirely behind you, to show that horrid woman who threw you over that you will make your life a success in spite of her. Rouse yourself, my dear Roger, and do your best. I hope by now you have forwarded *all* my introductions? You have your opportunity, and I must say you will be a great fool if you don't use it. *Do* use it my dear boy, for my sake. I am a very unhappy woman; but you might, if you would, bring back a little brightness to my life."

After he had read the letter, young Barnes sat for some time in a brown study on the edge of his bed. The letter contained only one more repetition of counsels that had been dinned into his ears for months—almost ever since the financial crash which had followed his father's death, and the crash of another sort, concerning himself, which had come so quick upon it. His thoughts returned, as they always did at some hour of the day or night, to the "horrid woman." Yes, that had hit him hard; the lad's heart still throbbed with bitterness as he thought of it. He had never felt anything so much; he didn't believe he should ever mind anything so much again. "I'm not one of your sentimental sort," he thought, half congratulating himself, half in self-contempt. But he could not get her out of his head; he wondered if he ever should. And it had gone pretty far too. By Jove! that night in the orchard!—when she had kissed him, and thrown her arms round his neck! And then to write him that letter, when things were at their worst. She might have done the thing decently. Have treated a fellow kindly at least. Well, of course, it was all done with. Yes, it *was*. Done with!

He got up and began to pace his small room, his hands in his pockets, thinking of the night in the orchard. Then gradually the smart lessened, and his thoughts passed away to other things. That little Yankee girl had really made good sport all the way home. He had not been dull for a moment; she had teased and provoked him so. Her eyes, too, were wonderfully pretty, and her small, pointed chin, and her witch-like imperious ways. Was it her money, the sense that she could do as she liked with most people, that made her so domineering and masterful? Very likely. On the journey he had put it down just to a natural and very surprising impudence. That was when he believed that she was a teacher, earning her bread. But the impudence had not prevented him from finding it much more amusing to talk to her than to anybody else.

And, on the whole, he thought she had not disliked him, though she had said the rudest things to him, and he had retaliated. She had asked him, indeed, to join them in an excursion the following day, and to tea at the Country Club. He had meant, if possible, to go back to New York on the morrow. But perhaps a day or two longer——

So she had a million—the little sprite? She was and would be a handful!—with a fortune or without it. And possessed also of the most extraordinary opinions. But he thought he would go on the excursion, and to the Country Club. He began to fold his mother's letter, and put it back into its envelope, while a slight flush mounted in his cheeks, and the young mouth that was still so boyish and candid took a stiffer line.

CHAPTER III

"Is Miss Floyd at home?"

The questioner was Mrs. Verrier, who had just alighted from her carriage at the door of the house in Columbia Avenue inhabited by Miss Floyd and her chaperon.

The maid replied that Miss Floyd had not yet returned, but had left a message begging Mrs. Verrier to wait for her. The visitor was accordingly ushered to the drawing-room on the first floor.

This room, the staircase, the maid, all bore witness to Miss Floyd's simplicity—like the Romney dress of Mount Vernon. The colour of the walls and the hangings, the lines of the furniture, were all subdued, even a little austere. Quiet greens and blues, mingled with white, showed the artistic mind; the chairs and sofas were a trifle stiff and straight legged; the electric fittings were of a Georgian plainness to match the Colonial architecture of the house; the beautiful self-coloured carpet was indeed Persian and costly, but it betrayed its costliness only to the expert. Altogether, the room, one would have said, of any *bourse moyenne*, with an eye for beauty. Fine photographs also, of Italian and Dutch pictures, suggested travel, and struck the cultivated cosmopolitan note.

Mrs. Verrier looked round it with a smile. It was all as unpretending as the maid who ushered her upstairs. Daphne would have no men-servants in her employ. What did two ladies want with them, in a democratic country? But Mrs. Verrier happened to know that Daphne's maid-servants were just as costly in their degree as the drawing-room carpet. Chosen for her in London with great care, attracted to Washington by enormous wages, these numerous damsels played their part in the general "simplicity" effect; but on the whole Mrs. Verrier believed that Daphne's household was rather more expensive than that of other rich people who employed men.

She walked through the room, looking absently at the various photographs and engravings, till her attention was excited by an easel and a picture upon it in the back drawing-room. She went up to it with a muttered exclamation.

"So *she* bought it! Daphne's amazing!"

For what she saw before her was a masterpiece—an excessively costly masterpiece—of the Florentine school, smuggled out of Italy, to the wrath of the Italian Government, some six months before this date, and since then lost to general knowledge. Rumour had given it first to a well-known collection at Boston; then to another at Philadelphia; yet here it was in the possession of a girl of two-and-twenty of whom the great world was just—but only just—beginning to talk.

"How like Daphne!" thought her friend with malice. The "simple" room, and the priceless picture carelessly placed in a corner of it, lest any one should really suppose that Daphne Floyd was an ordinary mortal.

Mrs. Verrier sat down at last in a chair fronting the picture and let herself fall into a reverie. On this occasion she was dressed in black. The lace strings of a hat crowned with black ostrich feathers were fastened under her chin by a diamond that sparkled in the dim greenish light of the drawing-room; the feathers of the hat were unusually large and drooping; they curled heavily round the thin neck and long, hollow-eyed face, so that its ivory whiteness, its fatigue, its fretful beauty were framed in and emphasized by them; her bloodless hands lay upon her lap, and the folds of the sweeping dress drawn round her showed her slenderness, or rather her emaciation. Two years before this date Madeleine Verrier had been a great beauty, and she had never yet reconciled herself to physical losses which were but the outward and visible sign of losses "far more deeply interfused." As she sat apparently absorbed in thought before the picture, she moved, half consciously, so that she could no longer see herself in a mirror opposite.

Yet her thoughts were in truth much engaged with Daphne and Daphne's proceedings. It was now nearly three weeks since Roger Barnes had appeared on the horizon. General Hobson had twice postponed his departure for England, and was still "enduring hardness" in a Washington hotel. Why his nephew should not be allowed to manage his courtship, if it was a courtship, for himself, Mrs. Verrier did not understand. There was no love lost between herself and the General, and she made much mock of him in her talks with Daphne. However, there he was; and she could only suppose that he took the situation seriously and felt bound to watch it in the interests of the young man's absent mother.

Was it serious? Certainly Daphne had been committing herself a good deal. The question was whether she had not been committing herself more than the young man had been doing on his side. That was the astonishing part of it. Mrs. Verrier could not sufficiently admire the skill with which Roger Barnes had so far played his part; could not sufficiently ridicule her own lack of insight, which at her first meeting with him had pronounced him stupid. Stupid he might be in the sense that it was of no use to expect from him the kind of talk on books, pictures, and first principles which prevailed in Daphne's circle. But Mrs. Verrier thought she had seldom come across a finer sense of tactics than young Barnes had so far displayed in his dealings with Daphne. If he went on as he had begun, the probability was that he would succeed.

Did she, Madeleine Verrier, wish him to succeed?

Daphne had grown tragically necessary to her, in this world of American society—in that section of it, at any rate, in which she desired to move, where the widow of Leopold Verrier was always conscious of the blowing of a cold and hostile breath. She was not excluded, but she was not welcome; she was not ostracized, but she had lost consideration. There had been something picturesque and appealing in her husband; something unbearably tragic in the manner of his death. She had braved it out by staying in America, instead of losing herself in foreign towns; and she had thereby proclaimed that she had no guilty sense of responsibility, no burden on her conscience; that she had only behaved as a thousand other women would have behaved, and without any cruel intention at all. But she knew all the same that the spectators of what had happened held her for a cruel woman, and that there were many, and those the best, who saw her come with distaste and go without regret; and it was under that knowledge, in spite of indomitable pride, that her beauty had withered in a year.

And at the moment when the smart of what had happened to her—personally and socially—was at its keenest; when, after a series of quarrels, she had separated herself from the imperious mother who had been her evil genius throughout her marriage, she had made friends, unexpectedly, owing to a chance meeting at a picture-gallery, with Daphne Floyd. Some element in Daphne's nature had attracted and disarmed her. The proud, fastidious woman had given the girl her confidence—eagerly, indiscriminately. She had poured out upon her all that wild philosophy of "rights" which is still struggling in the modern mind with a crumbling ethic and a vanishing religion. And she had found in Daphne a warm and passionate ally. Daphne was nothing if not "advanced." She shrank, as Roger Barnes had perceived, from no question; she had never been forbidden, had never forbidden herself, any book that she had a fancy to read; and she was as ready to discuss the relative divorce laws of Massachusetts and Pennsylvania, as the girls of fifty years ago were to talk of the fashions, or "Evangeline." In any disputed case, moreover, between a man and a woman, Daphne was hotly and instinctively on the side of the woman. She had thrown herself, therefore, with ardour into the defence of Mrs. Verrier; and for her it was not the wife's desertion, but the husband's suicide which had been the cruel and indefensible thing. All these various traits and liberalisms had made her very dear to Madeleine Verrier.

Now, as that lady sat in her usual drooping attitude, wondering what Washington would be like for her when even Daphne Floyd was gone from it, the afternoon sun stole through the curtains of the window on the street and touched some of the furniture and engravings in the inner drawing-room. Suddenly Mrs. Verrier started in her chair. A face had emerged thrown out upon the shadows by the sun-finger—the countenance of a handsome young Jew, as Rembrandt had once conceived it. Rare and high intelligence, melancholy, and premonition:—they were there embodied, so long as the apparition lasted.

The effect on Mrs. Verrier was apparently profound. She closed her eyes; her lips quivered; she leaned back feebly in her chair, breathing a name. The crisis lasted a few minutes, while the momentary vision faded and the sun-light crept on. The eyelids unclosed at last, slowly and painfully, as though shrinking from what might greet the eyes beneath them. But the farther wall was now in deep shade. Mrs. Verrier sat up; the emotion which had mastered her like a possession passed away; and rising hurriedly, she went back to the front drawing-room. She had hardly reached it when Miss Floyd's voice was heard upon the stairs.

Daphne entered the room in what appeared to be a fit of irritation. She was scolding the parlour-maid, whose high colour and dignified silence proclaimed her both blameless and long-suffering. At the sight of Mrs. Verrier Daphne checked herself with an effort and kissed her friend rather absently.

"Dear Madeleine!—very good of you to wait. Have they given you tea? I suppose not. My household seems to have gone mad this afternoon. Sit down. Some tea, Blount, at once."

Mrs. Verrier sank into a corner of the sofa, while Daphne, with an "ouf!" of fatigue, took off her hat, and threw herself down at the other end, her small feet curled up beneath her. Her half-frowning eyes gave the impression that she was still out of temper and on edge.

"Where have you been?" asked her companion quietly.

"Listening to a stuffy debate in the Senate," said Daphne without a smile.

"The Senate. What on earth took you there?"

"Well, why shouldn't I go?—why does one do anything? It was just a debate—horribly dull—trusts, or something of that kind. But there was a man attacking the President—and the place was crowded. Ugh! the heat was intolerable!"

"Who took you?"

Daphne named an under-secretary—an agreeable and ambitious man, who had been very much in her train during the preceding winter, and until Roger Barnes appeared upon the scene.

"I thought until I got your message that you were going to take Mr. Barnes motoring up the river."

"Mr. Barnes was engaged." Daphne gave the information tersely, rousing herself afterwards to make tea, which appeared at that moment.

"He seems to have been a good deal engaged this week," said Mrs. Verrier, when they were alone again.

Daphne made no reply. And Mrs. Verrier, after observing her for a moment, resumed:

"I suppose it was the Bostonians?"

"I suppose so. What does it matter?" The tone was dry and sharp.

"Daphne, you goose!" laughed Mrs. Verrier, "I believe this is the very first invitation of theirs he has accepted at all. He was written to about them by an old friend—his Eton master, or somebody of that sort. And as they turned up here on a visit, instead of his having to go and look for them at Boston, of course he had to call upon them."

"I dare say. And of course he had to go to tea with them yesterday, and he had to take them to Arlington this afternoon! I suppose I'd better tell you—we had a quarrel on the subject last night."

"Daphne!—don't, for heaven's sake, make him think himself too important!" cried Mrs. Verrier.

Daphne, with both elbows on the table, was slowly crunching a morsel of toast in her small white teeth. She had a look of concentrated energy—as of a person charged and overcharged with force of some kind, impatient to be let loose. Her black eyes sparkled; impetuosity and will shone from them; although they showed also rims of fatigue, as if Miss Daphne's nights had not of late been all they should be. Mrs. Verrier was chiefly struck, however, by the perception that for the first time Daphne was not having altogether her own way with the world. Madeleine had not observed anything of the same kind in her before. In general she was in entire command both of herself and of the men who surrounded her. She made a little court out of them, and treated them *en despote*. But Roger Barnes had not lent himself to the process; he had not played the game properly; and Daphne's sleep had been disturbed for the first time in history.

It had been admitted very soon between the two friends—without putting it very precisely—that Daphne was interested in Roger Barnes. Mrs. Verrier believed that the girl had been originally carried off her feet by the young man's superb good looks, and by the natural distinction—evident in all societies—which they conferred upon him. Then, no doubt, she had been piqued by his good-humoured, easy way—the absence of any doubt of himself, of tremor, of insistence. Mrs. Verrier said to herself—not altogether shrewdly—that he had no nerves, or no heart; and Daphne had not yet come across the genus. Her lovers had either possessed too much heart—like Captain Boyson—or a lack of coolness, when it really came to the point of grappling with Daphne and her millions, as in the case of a dozen she could name. Whereby it had come about that Daphne's attention had been first provoked, then peremptorily seized by the Englishman; and Mrs. Verrier began now to suspect that deeper things were really involved.

Certainly there was a good deal to puzzle the spectator. That the English are a fortune-hunting race may be a popular axiom; but it was quite possible, after all, that Roger Barnes was not the latest illustration of it. It was quite possible, also, that he had a sweetheart at home, some quiet, Quakerish girl who would never wave in his face the red flags that Daphne was fond of brandishing. It was equally possible that he was merely fooling with Daphne—that he had seen girls he liked better in New York, and was simply killing time till a sportsman friend of whom he talked should appear on the scene and take him off to shoot moose and catch trout in the province of Quebec. Mrs. Verrier realized that, for all his lack of subtlety and the higher conversation, young Barnes had managed astonishingly to keep his counsel. His "simplicity," like Daphne's, seemed to be of a special type.

And yet—there was no doubt that he had devoted himself a great deal. Washington society had quickly found him out; he had been invited to all the most fastidious houses, and was immensely in request for picnics and expeditions. But he had contrived, on the whole, to make all these opportunities promote the flirtation with Daphne. He had, in fact, been enough at her beck and call to make her the envy of a young society with whom the splendid Englishman promised to become the rage, and not enough to silence or wholly discourage other claimants on his time.

This no doubt accounted for the fact that the two charming Bostonians, Mrs. Maddison and her daughter, who had but lately arrived in Washington and made acquaintance with Roger Barnes, were still evidently in ignorance of what was going on. They were not initiated. They had invited young Barnes in the innocence of their hearts, without inviting Daphne Floyd, whom they did not previously know. And the young man had seen fit to accept their invitation. Hence the jealousy that was clearly burning in Daphne, that she was not indeed even trying to hide from the shrewd eyes of her friend.

Mrs. Verrier's advice not to make Roger Barnes "too important" had called up a flash of colour in the girl's cheeks. But she did not resent it in words; rather her silence deepened, till Mrs. Verrier stretched out a hand and laughingly turned the small face towards her that she might see what was in it.

"Daphne! I really believe you're in love with him!"

"Not at all," said Daphne, her eyelids flickering; "I never know what to talk to him about."

"As if that mattered!"

"Elsie Maddison always knows what to talk to him about, and he chatters to her the whole time."

Mrs. Verrier paused a moment, then said: "Do you suppose he came to America to marry money?"

"I haven't an idea."

"Do you suppose he knows that you—are not exactly a pauper?"

Daphne drew herself away impatiently. "I really don't suppose anything, Madeleine. He never talks about money, and I should think he had plenty himself."

Mrs. Verrier replied by giving an outline of the financial misfortunes of Mr. Barnes *père*, as they had been described to her by another English traveller in Washington.

Daphne listened indifferently. "He can't be very poor or he wouldn't behave as he does. And he is to inherit the General's property. He told me so."

"And it wouldn't matter to you, Daphne, if you did think a man had married you for money?"

Daphne had risen, and was pacing the drawing-room floor, her hands clasped behind her back. She turned a cloudy face upon her questioner. "It would matter a great deal, if I thought it had been only for money. But then, I hope I shouldn't have been such a fool as to marry him."

"But you could bear it, if the money counted for something?"

"I'm not an idiot!" said the girl, with energy. "With whom doesn't money count for something? Of course a man must take money into consideration." There was a curious touch of arrogance in the gesture which accompanied the words.

"'How pleasant it is to have money, heigh-ho!—How pleasant it is to have money,'" said Mrs. Verrier, quoting, with a laugh. "Yes, I dare say, you'd be very reasonable, Daphne, about that kind of thing. But I don't think you'd be a comfortable wife, dear, all the same."

"What do you mean?"

"You might allow your husband to spare a little love to your money; you would be for killing him if he ever looked at another woman!"

"You mean I should be jealous?" asked Daphne, almost with violence. "You are quite right there. I should be very jealous. On that point I should 'find quarrel in a straw.'"

Her cheeks had flushed a passionate red. The eyes which she had inherited from her Spanish grandmother blazed above them. She had become suddenly a woman of Andalusia and the South, moved by certain primitive forces in the blood.

Madeleine Verrier held out her hands, smiling.

"Come here, little wild cat. I believe you are jealous of Elsie Maddison."

Daphne approached her slowly, and slowly dropped into a seat beside her friend, her eyes still fixed and splendid. But as she looked into them Madeleine Verrier saw them suddenly dimmed.

"Daphne! you *are* in love with him!"

The girl recovered herself, clenching her small hands. "If I am," she said resolutely, "it is strange how like the other thing it is! I don't know whether I shall speak to him to-night."

"To-night?" Mrs. Verrier looked a little puzzled.

"At the White House. You're going, of course."

"No, I am not going." The voice was quiet and cold. "I am not asked."

Daphne, vexed with herself, touched her friend's hand caressingly. "It will be just a crush, dear. But I promised various people to go."

"And he will be there?"

"I suppose so." Daphne turned her head away, and then sprang up. "Have you seen the picture?"

Mrs. Verrier followed her into the inner room, where the girl gave a laughing and triumphant account of her acquisition, the agents she had employed, the skill with which it had been conveyed out of Italy, the wrath of various famous collectors, who had imagined that the fight lay between them alone, when they found the prize had been ravished from them. Madeleine Verrier was very intelligent, and the contrast, which the story brought out, between the girl's fragile youth and the strange and passionate sense of power which breathed from her whenever it became a question of wealth and the use of it, was at no point lost upon her companion.

Daphne would not allow any further talk of Roger Barnes. Her chaperon, Mrs. Phillips, presently appeared, and passed through rather a bad quarter of an hour while the imperious mistress of the house inquired into certain invitations and card-leavings that had not been managed to her liking. Then Daphne sat down to write a letter to a Girls' Club in New York, of which she was President—where, in fact, she occasionally took the Singing Class, with which she had made so much play at her first meeting with Roger Barnes. She had to tell them that she had just engaged a holiday house for them, to which they might go in instalments throughout the summer. She would pay the rent, provide a lady-superintendent, and make herself responsible for all but food expenses. Her small face relaxed—became quite soft and charming—as she wrote.

"But, my dear," cried Mrs. Phillips in dismay, as Daphne handed her the letter to read, "you have taken the house on Lake George, and you know the girls had all set their hearts on that place in the White Mountains!"

Daphne's lips tightened. "Certainly I have taken the house on Lake George," she said, as she carefully wiped her pen. "I told them I should."

"But, my dear, they are so tired of Lake George! They have been there three years running. And you know they subscribe a good deal themselves."

"Very well!—then let them do without my help. I have inquired into the matter. The house on Lake George is much more suitable than the White Mountains farm, and I have written to the agent. The thing's done."

Mrs. Phillips argued a little more, but Daphne was immovable.

Mrs. Verrier, watching the two, reflected, as she had often done before, that Mrs. Phillips's post was not particularly enviable. Daphne treated her in many ways with great generosity, paid her highly, grudged her no luxury, and was always courteous to her in public. But in private Daphne's will was law, and she had an abrupt and dictatorial way of asserting it that brought the red back into Mrs. Phillips's faded cheeks. Mrs. Verrier had often expected her to throw up her post. But there was no doubt something in Daphne's personality which made life beside her too full of colour to be lightly abandoned.

Daphne presently went upstairs to take off her walking-dress, and Mrs. Phillips, with a rather troubled face, began to tidy the confusion of letters she had left behind her.

"I dare say the girls won't mind," said Madeleine Verrier, kindly.

Mrs. Phillips started, and her mild lips quivered a little. Daphne's charities were for Daphne an amusement; for this gentle, faded woman, who bore all the drudgery of them, they were the chief attraction of life in Daphne's house. Mrs. Phillips loved the club-girls, and the thought of their disappointment pained her.

"I must try and put it to them," was her patient reply.

"Daphne must always have her way," Madeleine went on, smiling. "I wonder what she'll do when she marries."

Mrs. Phillips looked up quickly.

"I hope it'll be the right man, Mrs. Verrier. Of course, with anyone so—so clever—and so used to managing everything for herself—one would be a little anxious."

Mrs. Verrier's expression changed. A kind of wildness—fanaticism—invaded it, as of one recalling a mission. "Oh, well, nothing is irrevocable nowadays," she said, almost with violence. "Still I hope Daphne won't make a mistake."

Mrs. Phillips looked at her companion, at first in astonishment. Then a change passed over her face. With a cold excuse she left Mrs. Verrier alone.

CHAPTER IV

The reception at the White House was being given in honour of the delegates to a Peace Congress. The rooms were full without being inconveniently crowded and the charming house opened its friendly doors to a society more congruous and organic, richer also in the nobler kind of variety than America, perhaps, can offer to her guests elsewhere. What the opera and international finance are to New York, politics and administration are, as we all know, to Washington. And the visitor from Europe, conversationally starved for want of what seem to him the only topics worth discussing, finds himself within hearing once more of ministers, cabinets, embassies, and parliamentary gossip. Even General Hobson had come to admit that—especially for the middle-aged—Washington parties were extremely agreeable. The young and foolish might sigh for the flesh-pots of New York; those on whom "the black ox had trodden," who were at all aware what a vast tormenting, multitudinous, and headstrong world man has been given to inhabit; those who were engaged in governing any part of that world, or meant some day to be thus engaged; for them Washington was indispensable, and New York a mere entertainment.

Moreover Washington, at this time of the world's history, was the scene of one of those episodes—those brisker moments in the human comedy—which every now and then revive among us an almost forgotten belief in personality, an almost forgotten respect for the mysteries behind it. The guests streaming through the White House defiled past a man who, in a level and docketed world, appeared to his generation as the reincarnation of forces primitive, over-mastering, and heroic. An honest Odysseus!—toil-worn and storm-beaten, yet still with the spirit and strength, the many devices, of a boy; capable like his prototype in one short day of crushing his enemies, upholding his friends, purifying his house; and then, with the heat of righteous battle still upon him, with its gore, so to speak, still upon his hands, of turning his mind, without a pause and without hypocrisy, to things intimate and soft and pure—the domestic sweetness of Penelope, the young promise of Telemachus. The President stood, a rugged figure, amid the cosmopolitan crowd, breasting the modern world, like some ocean headland, yet not truly of it, one of the great fighters and workers of mankind, with a laugh that pealed above the noise, blue eyes that seemed to pursue some converse of their own, and a hand that grasped and cheered, where other hands withdrew and repelled. This one man's will had now, for some years, made the pivot on which vast issues turned—issues of peace and war, of policy embracing the civilized world; and, here, one saw him in drawing-rooms, discussing Alaric's campaigns with an Oxford professor, or chatting with a young mother about her children.

Beside him, the human waves, as they met and parted, disclosed a woman's face, modelled by nature in one of her lightest and deftest moods, a trifle detached, humorous also, as though the world's strange sights stirred a gentle and kindly mirth behind its sweet composure. The dignity of the President's wife was complete, yet it had not extinguished the personality it clothed; and where royalty, as the European knows it, would have donned its mask and stood on its defence, Republican royalty dared to be its amused, confiding, natural self.

All around—the political, diplomatic world of Washington. General Hobson, as he passed through it, greeted by what was now a large acquaintance, found himself driven once more to the inward confession—the grudging confession—as though Providence had not played him fair in extorting it—that American politicians were of a vastly finer stamp than he had expected to find them. The American press was all—he vowed—that fancy had painted it, and more. But, as he looked about him at the members of the President's administration—at this tall, black-haired man, for instance, with the mild and meditative eye, the equal, social or intellectual, of any Foreign Minister that Europe might pit against him, or any diplomat that might be sent to handle him; or this younger man, sparely built, with the sane, handsome face—son of a famous father, modest, amiable, efficient; or this other, of huge bulk and height, the sport of caricature, the hope of a party, smiling already a presidential smile as he passed, observed and beset, through the crowded rooms; or these naval or military men, with their hard serviceable looks, and the curt good manners of their kind:—the General saw as clearly as anybody else, that America need make no excuses whatever for her best men, that she has evolved the leaders she wants, and Europe has nothing to teach them.

He could only console himself by the remembrance of a speech, made by a well-known man, at a military function which the General had attended as a guest of honour the day before. There at last was the real thing! The real, Yankee, spread-eagle thing! The General positively hugged the thought of it.

"The American soldier," said the speaker, standing among the ambassadors, the naval and military *attachés*, of all the European nations, "is the superior of all other soldiers in three respects—bravery, discipline, intelligence."

Bravery, discipline, intelligence! Just those—the merest trifle! The General had found himself chuckling over it in the visions of the night.

Tired at last of these various impressions, acting on a mind not quite alert enough to deal with them, the General went in search of his nephew. Roger had been absent all day, and the General had left the hotel before his return. But the uncle was sure that he would sooner or later put in an appearance.

It was of course entirely on Roger's account that this unwilling guest of America was her guest still. For three weeks now had the General been watching the affair between Roger and Daphne Floyd. It had gone with such a rush at first, such a swing and fervour, that the General had felt that any day might bring the *dénouement*. It was really impossible to desert the lad at such a crisis, especially as Laura was so excitable and anxious, and so sure to make her brother pay for it if he failed to support her views and ambitions at the right moment. The General moreover felt the absolute necessity of getting to know something more about Miss Floyd, her character, the details of her fortune and antecedents, so that when the great moment came he might be prepared.

But the astonishing thing was that of late the whole affair seemed to have come to some stupid hitch! Roger had been behaving like a very cool hand—too cool by half in the General's opinion. What the deuce did he mean by hanging about these Boston ladies, if his affections were really fixed on Miss Daphne?—or his ambitions, which to the uncle seemed nearer the truth.

"Well, where is the nephew?" said Cecilia Boyson's voice in his ear.

The General turned. He saw a sharp, though still young face, a thin and willowy figure, attired in white silk, a *pince-nez* on the high-pitched nose, and a cool smile. Unconsciously his back stiffened. Miss Boyson invariably roused in him a certain masculine antagonism.

"I should be glad if you would tell me," he said, with some formality. "There are two or three people here to whom he should be introduced."

"Has he been picnicking with the Maddisons?" The voice was shrill, perhaps malicious.

"I believe they took him to Arlington, and somewhere else afterwards."

"Ah," said Cecilia, "there they are."

The General looked towards the door and saw his nephew enter, behind a mother and daughter whom, as it seemed to him, their acquaintances in the crowd around them greeted with a peculiar cordiality; the mother, still young, with a stag-like carriage of the head, a long throat, swathed in white tulle, and grizzled hair, on which shone a spray of diamonds; the daughter, equally tall and straight, repeating her mother's beauty with a bloom and radiance of her own. Innocent and happy, with dark eyes and a soft mouth, Miss Maddison dropped a little curtsey to the presidential pair, and the room turned to look at her as she did so.

"A very sweet-looking girl," said the General warmly. "Her father is, I think, a professor."

"He was. He is now just a writer of books. But Elsie was brought up in Cambridge. How did Mr. Roger know them?"

"His Eton tutor told him to go and see them."

"I thought Miss Floyd expected him to-day?" said Miss Boyson carelessly, adjusting her eyeglass.

"It was a mistake, a misunderstanding," replied the General hurriedly. "Miss Floyd's party is put off till next week."

"Daphne is just coming in," said Miss Boyson.

The General turned again. The watchful Cecilia was certain that *he* was not in love with Daphne. But the nephew—the inordinately handsome, and by now much-courted young man—what was the real truth about him?

Cecilia recognized—with Mrs. Verrier—that merely to put the question involved a certain tribute to young Barnes. He had at any rate done his fortune-hunting, if fortune-hunting it were, with decorum.

"Miss Floyd is looking well to-night," remarked the General.

Cecilia did not reply. She and a great part of the room were engaged in watching Roger Barnes and Miss Maddison walking together through a space which seemed to have been cleared on purpose for them, but was really the result of a move towards the supper-room.

"Was there ever such a pair?" said an enthusiastic voice behind the General. "Athene and Apollo take the floor!" A gray-haired journalist with a small, bewrinkled face, buried in whiskers, and beard, laid a hand on the General's arm as he spoke.

The General smiled vaguely. "Do you know Mrs. and Miss Maddison?"

"Rather!" said the little man. "Miss Elsie's a wonder! As pretty and soft as they make them, and a Greek scholar besides—took all sorts of honours at Radcliffe last year. I've known her from her cradle."

"What a number of your girls go to college!" said the General, but ungraciously, in the tones of one who no sooner saw an American custom emerging than his instinct was to hit it.

"Yes; it's a feature of our modern life—the life of our women. But not the most significant one, by a long way."

The General could not help a look of inquiry.

The journalist's face changed from gay to grave. "The most significant thing in American life just now——"

"I know!" interrupted the General. "Your divorce laws!"

The journalist shook his head. "It goes deeper than that. What we're looking on at is a complete transformation of the idea of marriage——"

A movement in the crowd bore the speaker away. The General was left watching the beautiful pair in the distance. They were apparently quite unconscious that they roused any special attention. Laughing and chatting like two children, they passed into the supper-room and disappeared.

Ten minutes later, in the supper-room, Barnes deserted the two ladies with whom he had entered, and went in pursuit of a girl in white, whose necklace of star sapphires, set in a Spanish setting of the seventeenth century, had at once caught the eye of the judicious. Roger, however, knew nothing of jewels, and was only conscious as he approached Miss Floyd, first of the mingling in his own mind of something like embarrassment with something like defiance, and then, of the glitter in the girl's dark eyes.

"I hope you had an interesting debate," he said. "Mrs. Phillips tells me you went to the Senate."

Daphne looked him up and down. "Did I?" she said slowly. "I've forgotten. Will you move, please? There's someone bringing me an ice." And turning her back on Roger, she smiled and beckoned to the Under-Secretary, who with a triumphant face was making his way to her through the crowd.

Roger coloured hotly. "May I bring Mrs. Maddison?" he said, passing her; "she would like to talk to you about a party for next week——"

"Thank you. I am just going home." And with an energetic movement she freed herself from him, and was soon in the gayest of talk with the Under-Secretary.

The reception broke up some time after midnight, and on the way home General Hobson attempted a raid upon his nephew's intentions.

"I don't wish to seem an intrusive person, my dear Roger, but may I ask how much longer you mean to stay in Washington?"

The tone was short and the look which accompanied the words not without sarcasm. Roger, who had been walking beside his companion, still deeply flushed, in complete silence, gave an awkward laugh.

"And as for you, Uncle Archie, I thought you meant to sail a fortnight ago. If you've been staying on like this on my account———"

"Don't make a fool either of me or yourself, Roger!" said the General hastily, roused at last to speech by the annoyance of the situation. "Of course it was on your account that I have stayed on. But what on earth it all means, and where your affairs are—I'm hanged if I have the glimmer of an idea!"

Roger's smile was perfectly good-humoured.

"I haven't much myself," he said quietly.

"Do you—or do you not—mean to propose to Miss Floyd?" cried the General, pausing in the centre of Lafayette Square, now all but deserted, and apostrophizing with his umbrella—for the night was soft and rainy—the presidential statue above his head.

"Have I given you reason to suppose that I was going to do so?" said Roger slowly.

"Given me?—given everybody reason?—of course you have!—a dozen times over. I don't like interfering with your affairs, Roger—with any young man's affairs—but you must know that you have set Washington talking, and it's not fair to a girl—by George it isn't!—when she has given you encouragement and you have made her conspicuous, to begin the same story, in the same place, immediately, with someone else! As you say, I ought to have taken myself off long ago."

"I didn't say anything of the kind," said Roger hotly; "you shouldn't put words into my mouth, Uncle Archie. And I really don't see why you attack me like this. My tutor particularly asked me, if I came across them, to be civil to Mrs. Maddison and her daughter, and I have done nothing but pay them the most ordinary attentions."

"When a man is in love he pays no ordinary attentions. He has eyes for no one but the lady." The General's umbrella, as it descended from the face of Andrew Jackson and rattled on the flagged path, supplied each word with emphasis. "However, it is no good talking, and I don't exactly know why I should put my old oar in. But the fact is I feel a certain responsibility. People here have been uncommonly civil. Well, well!—I've wired to-day to ask if there is a berth left in the *Venetia* for Saturday. And you, I suppose"—the inquiry was somewhat peremptory—"will be going back to New York?"

"I have no intention of leaving Washington just yet," said Roger, with decision.

"And may I ask what you intend to do here?"

Roger laughed. "I really think that's my business. However, you've been an awful brick, Uncle Archie, to stay on like this. I assure you, if I don't say much, I think it."

By this time they had reached the hotel, the steps and hall of which were full of people.

"That's how you put me off." The General's tone was resentful. "And you won't give me any idea of the line I am to take with your mother?"

The young man smiled again and waved an evasive hand.

"If you'll only be patient a little longer, Uncle Archie———"

At this point an acquaintance of the General's who was smoking in the hall came forward to greet him, and Roger made his escape.

Marriage à la mode

"Well, what the deuce *do* I mean to do?" Barnes asked himself the question deliberately. He was hanging out of the window, in his bedroom, smoking and pondering.

It was a mild and rainy night. Washington was full of the earth and leaf odours of the spring, which rose in gusts from its trees and gardens; and rugged, swiftly moving clouds disclosed every now and then what looked like hurrying stars.

The young man was excited and on edge. Daphne Floyd—and the thought of Daphne Floyd—had set his pulses hammering; they challenged in him the aggressive, self-assertive, masculine force. The history of the preceding three weeks was far from simple. He had first paid a determined court to her, conducting it in an orthodox, English, conspicuous way. His mother, and her necessities—his own also—imposed it on him; and he flung himself into it, setting his teeth. Then, to his astonishment, one may almost say to his disconcerting, he found the prey all at once, and, as it were, without a struggle, fluttering to his lure, and practically within his grasp. There was an evening when Daphne's sudden softness, the look in her eyes, the inflection in her voice had fairly thrown him off his balance. For the first time he had shown a lack of self-command and self-possession. Whereupon, in a flash, a new and strange Daphne had developed—imperious, difficult, incalculable. The more he gave, the more she claimed. Nor was it mere girlish caprice. The young Englishman, invited to a game that he had never yet played, felt in it something sinister and bewildering. Gropingly, he divined in front of him a future of tyranny on her side, of expected submission on his. The Northern character in him, with its reserve, its phlegm, its general sanity, began to shrink from the Southern elements in her. He became aware of the depths in her nature, of things volcanic and primitive, and the English stuff in him recoiled.

So he was to be bitted and bridled, it seemed, in the future. Daphne Floyd would have bought him with her dollars, and he would have to pay the price.

Something natural and wild in him said No! If he married this girl he would be master, in spite of her money. He realized vaguely, at any rate, the strength of her will, and the way in which it had been tempered and steeled by circumstance. But the perception only roused in himself some slumbering tenacities and vehemences of which he had been scarcely aware. So that, almost immediately—since there was no glamour of passion on his side—he began to resent her small tyrannies, to draw in, and draw back. A few quarrels—not ordinary lovers' quarrels, but representing a true grapple of personalities—sprang up behind a screen of trifles. Daphne was once more rude and provoking, Roger cool and apparently indifferent. This was the stage when Mrs. Verrier had become an admiring observer of what she supposed to be his "tactics." But she knew nothing of the curious little crisis which had preceded them.

Then the Maddisons, mother and daughter, "my tutor's friends," had appeared upon the scene—charming people! Of course civilities were due to them, and had to be paid them. Next to his mother—and to the girl of the orchard—the affections of this youth, who was morally backward and immature, but neither callous nor fundamentally selfish, had been chiefly given to a certain Eton master, of a type happily not uncommon in English public schools. Herbert French had been Roger's earliest and best friend. What Roger had owed him at school, only he knew. Since school-days they had been constant correspondents, and French's influence on his pupil's early manhood had done much, for all Roger's laziness and self-indulgence, to keep him from serious lapses.

Neglect any friends of his—and such jolly friends? Rather not! But as soon as Daphne had seen Elsie Maddison, and he had begged an afternoon to go on an expedition with them, Daphne had become intolerable. She had shown her English friend and his acquaintances a manner so insulting and provocative, that the young man's blood had boiled.

If he were in love with her—well and good! She might no doubt have tamed him by these stripes. But she was no goddess to him; no golden cloud enveloped her; he saw her under a common daylight. At the same time she attracted him; he was vain of what had seemed his conquest, and uneasily exultant in the thought of her immense fortune. "I'll make her an excellent husband if she marries me," he said to himself stubbornly; "I can, and I will."

But meanwhile how was this first stage to end? At the White House that night Daphne had treated him with contumely, and before spectators. He must either go or bring her to the point.

He withdrew suddenly from the window, flinging out the end of his cigarette. "I'll propose to her to-morrow—and she may either take me or leave me!"

He paced up and down his room, conscious of relief and fresh energy. As he did so his eyes were drawn to a letter from Herbert French lying on the table. He took it up and read it again—smiling over it broadly, in a boyish and kindly amusement. "By Jove! he's happy."

Then as he put it down his face darkened. There was something in the letter, in its manliness and humour, its unconscious revelation of ideals wholly independent of dollars, that made Roger for the moment loathe his own position. But he pulled himself together.

"I shall make her a good husband," he repeated, frowning. "She'll have nothing to complain of."

On the following day a picnic among the woods of the Upper Potomac brought together most of the personages in this history. The day was beautiful, the woods fragrant with spring leaf and blossom, and the stream, swollen with rain, ran seaward in a turbid, rejoicing strength.

The General, having secured his passage home, was in good spirits as far as his own affairs were concerned, though still irritable on the score of his nephew's. Since the abortive attempt on his confidence of the night before, Roger had avoided all private conversation with his uncle; and for once the old had to learn patience from the young.

The party was given by the wife of one of the staff of the French Embassy—a young Frenchwoman, as gay and frank as her babies, and possessed, none the less, of all the social arts of her nation. She had taken a shrewd interest in the matter of Daphne Floyd and the Englishman. Daphne, according to her, should be promptly married and her millions taken care of, and the handsome, broad-shouldered fellow impressed the little Frenchwoman's imagination as a proper and capable watchdog. She had indeed become aware that something was wrong, but her acuteness entirely refused to believe that it had any vital connection with the advent of pretty Elsie Maddison. Meanwhile, to please Daphne, whom she liked, while conscious of a strong and frequent desire to smite her, Madame de Fronsac had invited Mrs. Verrier, treating her with a cold and punctilious courtesy that, as applied to any other guest, would have seemed an affront.

In vain, however, did the hostess, in vain did other kindly bystanders, endeavour to play the game of Daphne Floyd. In the first place Daphne herself, though piped unto, refused to dance. She avoided the society of Roger Barnes in a pointed and public way, bright colour on her cheeks and a wild light in her eyes; the Under-Secretary escorted her and carried her wrap. Washington did not know what to think. For owing to this conduct of Daphne's, the charming Boston girl, the other *ingénue* of the party, fell constantly to the care of young Barnes; and to see them stepping along the green ways together, matched almost in height, and clearly of the same English ancestry and race, pleased while it puzzled the spectators.

The party lunched in a little inn beside the river, and then scattered again along woodland paths. Daphne and the Under-Secretary wandered on ahead and were some distance from the rest of the party when that gentleman suddenly looked at his watch in dismay. An appointment had to be kept with the President at a certain hour, and the Under-Secretary's wits had been wandering. There was nothing for it but to take a short cut through the woods to a local station and make at once for Washington.

Daphne quickened his uneasiness and hastened his departure. She assured him that the others were close behind, and that nothing could suit her better than to rest on a mossy stone that happily presented itself till they arrived.

The Under-Secretary, transformed into the anxious and ambitious politician, abruptly left her.

Daphne, as soon as he was gone, allowed herself the natural attitude that fitted her thoughts. She was furiously in love and torn with jealousy; and that love and jealousy could smart so, and cling so, was a strange revelation to one accustomed to make a world entirely to her liking. Her dark eyes were hollow, her small mouth had lost its colour, and she showed that touch of something wasting and withering that Theocritan shepherds knew in old Sicilian days. It was as though she had defied a god—and the god had avenged himself.

Suddenly he appeared—the teasing divinity—in human shape. There was a rustling among the brushwood fringing the river. Roger Barnes emerged and made his way up towards her.

"I've been stalking you all this time," he said, breathless, as he reached her, "and now at last—I've caught you!"

Daphne rose furiously. "What right have you to stalk me, as you call it—to follow me—to speak to me even? I wish to avoid you—and I have shown it!"

Roger looked at her. He had thrown down his hat, and she saw him against the background of sunny wood, as the magnificent embodiment of its youth and force. "And why have you shown it?" There was a warning tremor of excitement in his voice. "What have I done? I haven't deserved it! You treat me like—like a friend!—and then you drop me like a hot coal. You've been awfully unkind to me!"

"I won't discuss it with you," she cried passionately. "You are in my way, Mr. Barnes. Let me go back to the others!" And stretching out a small hand, she tried to put him aside.

Roger hesitated, but only for a moment. He caught the hand, he gathered its owner into a pair of strong arms, and bending over her, he kissed her. Daphne, suffocated with anger and emotion, broke from him—tottering. Then sinking on the ground beneath a tree, she burst into sobbing. Roger, scarlet, with sparkling eyes, dropped on one knee beside her.

"He caught the hand, he gathered its owner into a pair of strong arms, and bending over her, he kissed her"

"Daphne, I'm a ruffian! forgive me! you must, Daphne! Look here, I want you to marry me. I've nothing to offer you, of course; I'm a poor man, and you've all this horrible money! But I—I love you!—and I'll make you a good husband, Daphne, that I'll swear. If you'll take me, you shall never be sorry for it."

He looked at her again, sorely embarrassed, hating himself, yet inwardly sure of her. Her small frame shook with weeping. And presently she turned from him and said in a fierce voice:

"Go and tell all that to Elsie Maddison!"

Infinitely relieved, Roger gave a quick, excited laugh.

"She'd soon send me about my business! I should be a day too late for the fair, in *that* quarter. What do you think she and I have been talking about all this time, Daphne?"

"I don't care," said Daphne hastily, with face still averted.

"I'm going to tell you, all the same," cried Roger triumphantly, and diving into his coat pocket he produced "my tutor's letter." Daphne sat immovable, and he had to read it aloud himself. It contained the rapturous account of Herbert French's engagement to Miss Maddison, a happy event which had taken place in England during the Eton holidays, about a month before this date.

"There!" cried the young man as he finished it. "And she's talked about nothing all the time, nothing at all—but old Herbert—and how good he is—and how good-looking, and the Lord knows what! I got precious sick of it, though I think he's a trump, too. Oh, Daphne!—you were a little fool!"

"All the same, you have behaved abominably!" Daphne said, still choking.

"No, I haven't," was Roger's firm reply. "It was you who were so cross. I couldn't tell you anything. I say! you do know how to stick pins into people!"

But he took up her hand and kissed it as he spoke.

Daphne allowed it. Her breast heaved as the storm departed. And she looked so charming, so soft, so desirable, as she sat there in her white dress, with her great tear-washed eyes and fluttering breath, that the youth was really touched and carried off his feet; and the rest of his task was quite easy. All the familiar things that had to be said were said, and with all the proper emphasis and spirit. He played his part, the spring woods played theirs, and Daphne, worn out by emotion and conquered by passion, gradually betrayed herself wholly. And so much at least may be said to the man's credit that there were certainly moments in the half-hour between them when, amid the rush of talk, laughter, and caresses, that conscience which he owed so greatly to the exertions of "my tutor" pricked him not a little.

After losing themselves deliberately in the woods, they strolled back to join the rest of the party. The sounds of conversation were already audible through the trees in front of them, when they saw Mrs. Verrier coming towards them. She was walking alone and did not perceive them. Her eyes were raised and fixed, as though on some sight in front of them. The bitterness, the anguish, one might almost call it, of her expression, the horror in the eyes, as of one ghost-led, ghost-driven, drew an exclamation from Roger.

"There's Mrs. Verrier! Why, how ill she looks!"

Daphne paused, gazed, and shrank. She drew him aside through the trees.

"Let's go another way. Madeleine's often strange." And with a superstitious pang she wished that Madeleine Verrier's face had not been the first to meet her in this hour of her betrothal.

PART II

THREE YEARS AFTER

CHAPTER V

In the drawing-room at Heston Park two ladies were seated. One was a well-preserved woman of fifty, with a large oblong face, good features, a double chin, and abundant gray hair arranged in waved *bandeaux* above a forehead which should certainly have implied strength of character, and a pair of challenging black eyes. Lady Barnes moved and spoke with authority; it was evident that she had been accustomed to do so all her life; to trail silk gowns over Persian carpets, to engage expensive cooks and rely on expensive butlers, with a strict attention to small economies all the time; to impose her will on her household and the clergyman of the parish; to give her opinions on books, and expect them to be listened to; to abstain from politics as unfeminine, and to make up for it by the strongest of views on Church questions. She belonged to an English type common throughout all classes—quite harmless and tolerable when things go well, but apt to be soured and twisted by adversity.

And Lady Barnes, it will be remembered, had known adversity. Not much of it, nor for long together; but in her own opinion she had gone through "great trials," to the profit of her Christian character. She was quite certain, now, that everything had been for the best, and that Providence makes no mistakes. But that, perhaps, was because the "trials" had only lasted about a year; and then, so far as they were pecuniary, the marriage of her son with Miss Daphne Floyd had entirely relieved her of them. For Roger now made her a handsome allowance and the chastened habits of a most uncomfortable year had been hastily abandoned.

Nevertheless, Lady Barnes's aspect on this autumn afternoon was not cheerful, and her companion was endeavouring, with a little kind embarrassment, both to soothe an evident irritation and to avoid the confidences that Roger's mother seemed eager to pour out. Elsie French, whom Washington had known three years before as Elsie Maddison, was in that bloom of young married life when all that was lovely in the girl seems to be still lingering, while yet love and motherhood have wrought once more their old transforming miracle on sense and spirit. In her afternoon dress of dainty sprigged silk, with just a touch of austerity in the broad muslin collar and cuffs—her curly brown hair simply parted on her brow, and gathered classically on a shapely head—her mouth a little troubled, her brow a little puckered over Lady Barnes's discontents—she was a very gracious vision. Yet behind the gentleness, as even Lady Barnes knew, there were qualities and characteristics of a singular strength.

Lady Barnes indeed was complaining, and could not be stopped.

"You see, dear Mrs. French," she was saying, in a rapid, lowered voice, and with many glances at the door, "the trouble is that Daphne is never satisfied. She has some impossible ideal in her mind, and then everything must be sacrificed to it. She began with going into ecstasies over this dear old house, and now!—there's scarcely a thing in it she does not want to change. Poor Edward and I spent thousands upon it, and we really flattered ourselves that we had some taste; but it is not good enough for Daphne!"

The speaker settled herself in her chair with a slight but emphatic clatter of bangles and rustle of skirts.

"It's the ceilings, isn't it?" murmured Elsie French, glancing at the heavy decoration, the stucco bosses and pendants above her head which had replaced, some twenty years before, a piece of Adam design, sparing and felicitous.

"It's everything!" Lady Barnes's tone was now more angry than fretful. "I don't, of course, like to say it—but really Daphne's self-confidence is too amazing!"

"She does know so much," said Elsie French reflectively. "Doesn't she?"

"Well, if you call it knowing. She can always get some tiresome person, whom she calls an 'expert,' to back her up. But I believe in liking what you *do* like, and not being bullied into what you don't like."

"I suppose if one studies these things——" Elsie French began timidly.

"What's the good of studying!" cried Lady Barnes; "one has one's own taste, or one hasn't."

Confronted with this form of the Absolute, Elsie French looked perplexed; especially as her own artistic sympathies were mainly with Daphne. The situation was certainly awkward. At the time of the Barnes's financial crash, and Sir Edward Barnes's death, Heston Park, which belonged to Lady Barnes, was all that remained to her and her son. A park of a hundred acres and a few cottages went with the house; but there was no estate to support it, and it had to be let, to provide an income for the widow and the boy. Much of the expensive furniture had been sold before letting, but enough remained to satisfy the wants of a not very exacting tenant.

Lady Barnes had then departed to weep in exile on a pittance of about seven hundred a year. But with the marriage of her son to Miss Floyd and her millions, the mother's thoughts had turned fondly back to Heston Park. It was too big for her, of course; but the young people clearly must redeem it, and settle there. And Daphne had been quite amenable. The photographs charmed her. The house, she said, was evidently in a pure style, and it would be a delight to make it habitable again. The tenant, however, had a lease, and refused to turn out until at last Daphne had frankly bribed him to go. And now, after three years of married life, during which the young couple had rented various "places," besides their house in London and a villa at Tunis, Heston Park had been vacated, Daphne and Roger had descended upon it as Lady Barnes's tenants at a high rent, intent upon its restoration; and Roger's mother had been invited to their councils.

Hence, indeed, these tears. When Daphne first stepped inside the ancestral mansion of the Trescoes—such had been Lady Barnes's maiden name—she had received a severe shock. The outside, the shell of the house—delightful! But inside!—heavens! what taste, what decoration—what ruin of a beautiful thing! Half the old mantelpieces gone, the ceilings spoiled, the decorations "busy," pretentious, overdone, and nothing left to console her but an ugly row of bad Lelys and worse Highmores—the most despicable collection of family portraits she had ever set eyes upon!

Roger had looked unhappy. "It was father and mother did it," he admitted penitently. "But after all, Daphne, you know they *are* Trescoes!"—this with a defensive and protecting glance at the Lelys.

Daphne was sorry for it. Her mouth tightened, and certain lines appeared about it which already prophesied what the years would make of the young face. Yet it was a pretty mouth—the mouth, above all, of one with no doubts at all as to her place and rights in the world. Lady Barnes had pronounced it "common" in her secret thoughts before she had known its owner six weeks. But the adjective had never yet escaped the "bulwark of the teeth." Outwardly the mother and daughter-in-law were still on good terms. It was indeed but a week since the son and his wife had arrived—with their baby girl—at Heston Park, after a summer of yachting and fishing in Norway; since Lady Barnes had journeyed thither from London to meet them; and Mr. and Mrs. French had accepted an urgent invitation from Roger, quite sufficiently backed by Daphne, to stay for a few days with Mr. French's old pupil, before the reopening of Eton.

During that time there had been no open quarrels of any kind; but Elsie French was a sensitive creature, and she had been increasingly aware of friction and annoyance behind the scenes. And now here was Lady Barnes let loose! and Daphne might appear at any moment, before she could be re-caged.

"She puts you down so!" cried that lady, making gestures with the paper-knife she had just been employing on the pages of a Mudie book. "If I tell her that something or other—it doesn't matter what—cost at least a great deal of money, she has a way of smiling at you that is positively insulting! She doesn't trouble to argue; she begins to laugh, and raises her eyebrows. I—I always feel as if she had struck me in the face! I know I oughtn't to speak like this; I hadn't meant to do it, especially to a country-woman of hers, as you are."

"Am I?" said Elsie, in a puzzled voice.

Lady Barnes opened her eyes in astonishment.

"I meant"—the explanation was hurried—"I thought—Mrs. Barnes was a South American? Her mother was Spanish, of course; you see it in Daphne."

"Yes; in her wonderful eyes," said Mrs. French warmly; "and her grace—isn't she graceful! My husband says she moves like a sea-wave. She has given her eyes to the child."

"Ah! and other things too, I'm afraid!" cried Lady Barnes, carried away. "But here is the baby."

For the sounds of a childish voice were heard echoing in the domed hall outside. Small feet came pattering, and the drawing-room door was burst open by Roger Barnes, holding a little girl of nearly two and a half by the hand.

Lady Barnes composed herself. It is necessary to smile at children, and she endeavoured to satisfy her own sense of it.

"Come in, Beatty; come and kiss granny!" And Lady Barnes held out her arms.

But the child stood still, surveyed her grandmother with a pair of startling eyes, and then, turning, made a rush for the door. But her father was too quick for her. He closed it with a laugh, and stood with his back to it. The child did not cry, but, with flaming cheeks, she began to beat her father's knees with her small fists.

"Go and kiss granny, darling," said Roger, stroking her dark head.

Beatty turned again, put both her hands behind her, and stood immovable.

"Not kiss granny," she said firmly. "Don't love granny."

"Oh, Beatty"—Mrs. French knelt down beside her—"come and be a good little girl, and I'll show you picture-books."

"I not Beatty—I Jemima Ann," said the small thin voice. "Not be a dood dirl—do upstairs."

She looked at her father again, and then, evidently perceiving that he was not to be moved by force, she changed her tactics. Her delicate, elfish face melted into the sweetest smile; she stood on tiptoe, holding out to him her tiny arms. With a laugh of irrepressible pride and pleasure, Roger stooped to her and lifted her up. She nestled on his shoulder—a small Odalisque, dark, lithe, and tawny, beside her handsome, fair-skinned father. And Roger's manner of holding and caressing her showed the passionate affection with which he regarded her.

He again urged her to kiss her grandmother; but the child again shook her head. "Then," said he craftily, "father must kiss granny." And he began to cross the room.

But Lady Barnes stopped him, not without dignity. "Better not press it, Roger: another time."

Barnes laughed, and yielded. He carried the child away, murmuring to her, "Naughty, naughty 'ittie girl!" a remark which Beatty, tucked under his ear, and complacently sucking her thumb, received with complete indifference.

"There, you see!" said the grandmother, with slightly flushed cheeks, as the door closed: "the child has been already taught to dislike me, and if Roger had attempted to kiss me, she would probably have struck me."

"Oh, no!" cried Mrs. French. "She is a loving little thing."

"Except when she is jealous," said Lady Barnes, with significance. "I told you she has inherited more than her eyes."

Mrs. French rose. She was determined not to discuss her hostess any more, and she walked over to the bow window as though to look at the prospects of the weather, which had threatened rain. But Roger's mother was not to be repressed. Resentment and antagonism, nurtured on a hundred small incidents and trifling jars, and, to begin with, a matter of temperament, had come at last to speech. And in this charming New Englander, the wife of Roger's best friend, sympathetic, tender, with a touch in her of the nun and the saint, Lady Barnes could not help trying to find a supporter. She was a much weaker person than her square build and her double chin would have led the bystander to suppose; and her feelings had been hurt.

So that when Mrs. French returned to say that the sun seemed to be coming out, her companion, without heeding, went on, with emotion: "It's my son I am thinking of, Mrs. French. I know you're safe, and that Roger depends upon Mr. French more than upon anyone else in the world, so I can't help just saying a word to you about my anxiety. You know, when Roger married, I don't think he was much in love—in fact, I'm sure he wasn't. But now—it's quite different. Roger has a very soft heart, and he's very domestic. He was always the best of sons to me, and as soon as he was married he became the best of husbands. He's devoted to Daphne now, and you see how he adores the child. But the fact is, there's a person in this neighbourhood" (Lady Barnes lowered her voice and looked round her)—"I only knew it for certain this morning—who ... well, who might make trouble. And Daphne's temper is so passionate and uncontrolled that——"

"Dear Lady Barnes, please don't tell me any secrets!" Elsie French implored, and laid a restraining hand on the mother's arm, ready, indeed, to take up her work and fly. But Lady Barnes's chair stood between her and the door, and the occupant of it was substantial.

Laura Barnes hesitated, and in the pause two persons appeared upon the garden path outside, coming towards the open windows of the drawing-room. One was Mrs. Roger Barnes; the other was a man, remarkably tall and slender, with a stoop like that of an overgrown schoolboy, silky dark hair and moustache, and pale gray eyes.

"Dr. Lelius!" said Elsie, in astonishment. "Was Daphne expecting him?"

"Who is Dr. Lelius?" asked Lady Barnes, putting up her eyeglass.

Mrs. French explained that he was a South German art-critic, from Würzburg, with a great reputation. She had already met him at Eton and at Oxford.

"Another expert!" said Lady Barnes with a shrug.

The pair passed the window, absorbed apparently in conversation. Mrs. French escaped. Lady Barnes was left to discontent and solitude.

But the solitude was not for long.

When Elsie French descended for tea, an hour later, she was aware, from a considerable distance, of people and tumult in the drawing-room. Daphne's soprano voice—agreeable, but making its mark always, like its owner—could be heard running on. The young mistress of the house seemed to be admonishing, instructing, someone. Could it be her mother-in-law?

When Elsie entered, Daphne was walking up and down in excitement.

"One cannot really live with bad pictures because they happen to be one's ancestors! We won't do them any harm, mamma! of course not. There is a room upstairs where they can be stored—most carefully—and anybody who is interested in them can go and look at them. If they had only been left as they were painted!—not by Lely, of course, but by some drapery man in his studio—*passe encore*! they might have been just bearable. But you see some wretched restorer went and daubed them all over a few years ago."

"We went to the best man we could find! We took the best advice!" cried Lady Barnes, sitting stiff and crimson in a deep arm-chair, opposite the luckless row of portraits that Daphne was denouncing.

"I'm sure you did. But then, you see, nobody knew anything at all about it in those days. The restorers were all murderers. Ask Dr. Lelius."

Daphne pointed to the stranger, who was leaning against an arm-chair beside her in an embarrassed attitude, as though he were endeavouring to make the chair a buffer between himself and Lady Barnes.

Dr. Lelius bowed.

"It is a modern art," he said with diffidence, and an accent creditably slight—"a quite modern art. We hafe a great man at Würzburg."

"I don't suppose he professes to know anything about English pictures, does he?" asked Lady Barnes with scorn.

"Ach!—I do not propose that Mrs. Barnes entrust him wid dese pictures, Madame. It is now too late."

And the willowy German looked, with a half-repressed smile, at the row of pictures—all staring at the bystander with the same saucer eyes, the same wooden arms, and the same brilliance of modern paint and varnish, which not even the passage of four years since it was applied had been able greatly to subdue.

Lady Barnes lifted shoulders and eyes—a woman's angry protest against the tyranny of knowledge.

"All the same, they are my forbears, my kith and kin," she said, with emphasis. "But of course Mrs. Barnes is mistress here: I suppose she will do as she pleases."

The German stared politely at the carpet. It was now Daphne's turn to shrug. She threw herself into a chair, with very red cheeks, one foot hanging over the other, and the fingers of her hands, which shone with diamonds, tapping the chair impatiently. Her dress of a delicate pink, touched here and there with black, her wide black hat, and the eyes which glowed from the small pointed face beneath it; the tumbling masses of her dark hair as contrasted with her general lightness and slenderness; the red of the lips, the whiteness of the hands and brow, the dainty irregularity of feature: these things made a Watteau sketch of her, all pure colour and lissomeness, with dots and scratches of intense black. Daphne was much handsomer than she had been as a girl, but also a trifle less refined. All her points were intensified—her eyes had more flame; the damask of her cheek was deeper; her grace was wilder, her voice a little shriller than of old.

While the uncomfortable silence which the two women had made around them still lasted, Roger Barnes appeared on the garden steps.

"Hullo! any tea going?" He came in, without waiting for an answer, looked from his mother to Daphne, from Daphne to his mother, and laughed uncomfortably.

"Still bothering about those beastly pictures?" he said as he helped himself to a cup of tea.

"*Thank* you, Roger!" said Lady Barnes.

"I didn't mean any harm, mother." He crossed over to her and sat down beside her. "I say, Daphne, I've got an idea. Why shouldn't mother have them? She's going to take a house, she says. Let's hand them all over to her!"

Lady Barnes's lips trembled with indignation. "The Trescoes who were born and died in this house, belong here!" The tone of the words showed the stab to feeling and self-love. "It would be a sacrilege to move them."

"Well then, let's move ourselves!" exclaimed Daphne, springing up. "We can let this house again, can't we, Roger?"

"We can, I suppose," said Roger, munching his bread and butter; "but we're not going to."

He raised his head and looked quietly at her.

"I think we'd better!" The tone was imperious. Daphne, with her thin arms and hands locked behind her, paused beside her husband.

Dr. Lelius, stealthily raising his eyes, observed the two. A strange little scene—not English at all. The English, he understood, were a phlegmatic people. What had this little Southerner to do among them? And what sort of fellow was the husband?

It was evident that some mute coloquy passed between the husband and wife—disapproval on his part, attempt to assert authority, defiance, on hers. Then the fair-skinned English face, confronting Daphne, wavered and weakened, and Roger smiled into the eyes transfixing him.

"Ah!" thought Lelius, "she has him, de poor fool!"

Roger, coming over to his mother, began a murmured conversation. Daphne, still breathing quick, consented to talk to Dr. Lelius and Mrs. French. Lelius, who travelled widely, had brought her news of some pictures in a chateau of the Bourbonnais—pictures that her whole mind was set on acquiring. Elsie French noticed the *expertise* of her talk; the intellectual development it implied; the passion of will which accompanied it. "To the dollar, all things are possible"—one might have phrased it so.

The soft September air came in through the open windows, from a garden flooded with western sun. Suddenly through the subdued talk which filled the drawing-room—each group in it avoiding the other—the sound of a motor arriving made itself heard.

"Heavens! who on earth knows we're here?" said Barnes, looking up.

For they had only been camping a week in the house, far too busy to think of neighbours. They sat expectant and annoyed, reproaching each other with not having told the butler to say "Not at home." Lady Barnes's attitude had in it something else—a little anxiety; but it escaped notice. Steps came through the hall, and the butler, throwing open the door, announced—

"Mrs. Fairmile."

Roger Barnes sprang to his feet. His mother, with a little gasp, caught him by the arm instinctively. There was a general rise and a movement of confusion, till the new-comer, advancing, offered her hand to Daphne.

"I am afraid, Mrs. Barnes, I am disturbing you all. The butler told me you had only been here a few days. But Lady Barnes and your husband are such old friends of mine that, as soon as I heard—through our old postmistress, I think—that you had arrived, I thought I might venture."

The charming voice dropped, and the speaker waited, smiling, her eyes fixed on Daphne. Daphne had taken her hand in some bewilderment, and was now looking at her husband for assistance. It was clear to Elsie French, in the background, that Daphne neither knew the lady nor the lady's name, and that the visit had taken her entirely by surprise.

Barnes recovered himself quickly. "I had no idea you were in these parts," he said, as he brought a chair forward for the visitor, and stood beside her a moment.

Lady Barnes, observing him, as she stiffly greeted the new-comer—his cool manner, his deepened colour—felt the usual throb of maternal pride in him, intensified by alarm and excitement.

"Oh, I am staying a day or two with Duchess Mary," said the new-comer. "She is a little older—and no less gouty, poor dear, than she used to be. Mrs. Barnes, I have heard a great deal of you—though you mayn't know anything about me. Ah! Dr. Lelius?"

The German, bowing awkwardly, yet radiant, came forward to take the hand extended to him.

"They did nothing but talk about you at the Louvre, when I was there last week," she said, with a little confidential nod. "You have made them horribly uncomfortable about some of their things. Isn't it a pity to know too much?"

She turned toward Daphne. "I'm afraid that's your case too." She smiled, and the smile lit up a face full of delicate lines and wrinkles, which no effort had been made to disguise; a tired face, where the eyes spoke from caverns of shade, yet with the most appealing and persuasive beauty.

"Do you mean about pictures?" said Daphne, a little coldly. "I don't know as much as Dr. Lelius."

Humour leaped into the eyes fixed upon her; but Mrs. Fairmile only said: "That's not given to the rest of us mortals. But after all, *having's* better than knowing. Don't—*don't* you possess the Vitali Signorelli?"

Her voice was most musical and flattering. Daphne smiled in spite of herself. "Yes, we do. It's in London now—waiting till we can find a place for it."

"You must let me make a pilgrimage—when it comes. But you know you'd find a number of things at Upcott—where I'm staying now—that would interest you. I forget whether you've met the Duchess?"

"This is our first week here," said Roger, interposing. "The house has been let till now. We came down to see what could be made of it."

His tone was only just civil. His mother, looking on, said to herself that he was angry—and with good reason.

But Mrs. Fairmile still smiled.

"Ah! the Lelys!" she cried, raising her hand slightly toward the row of portraits on the wall. "The dear impossible things! Are you still discussing them—as we used to do?"

Daphne started. "You know this house, then?"

The smile broadened into a laugh of amusement, as Mrs. Fairmile turned to Roger's mother.

"Don't I, dear Lady Barnes—don't I know this house?"

Lady Barnes seemed to straighten in her chair. "Well, you were here often enough to know it," she said abruptly. "Daphne, Mrs. Fairmile is a distant cousin of ours."

"Distant, but quite enough to swear by!" said the visitor, gaily. "Yes, Mrs. Barnes, I knew this house very well in old days. It has many charming points." She looked round with a face that had suddenly become coolly critical, an embodied intelligence.

Daphne, as though divining for the first time a listener worthy of her steel, began to talk with some rapidity of the changes she wished to make. She talked with an evident desire to show off, to make an impression. Mrs. Fairmile listened attentively, occasionally throwing in a word of criticism or comment, in the softest, gentlest voice. But somehow, whenever she spoke, Daphne felt vaguely irritated. She was generally put slightly in the wrong by her visitor, and Mrs. Fairmile's extraordinary knowledge of Heston Park, and of everything connected with it, was so odd and disconcerting. She had a laughing way, moreover, of appealing to Roger Barnes himself to support a recollection or an opinion, which presently produced a contraction of Daphne's brows. Who was this woman? A cousin—a cousin who knew every inch of the house, and seemed to be one of Roger's closest friends? It was really too strange that in all these years Roger should never have said a word about her!

The red mounted in Daphne's cheek. She began, moreover, to feel herself at a disadvantage to which she was not accustomed. Dr. Lelius, meanwhile, turned to Mrs. Fairmile, whenever she was allowed to speak, with a joyous yet inarticulate deference he had never shown to his hostess. They understood each other at a word or a glance. Beside them Daphne, with all her cleverness, soon appeared as a child for whom one makes allowances.

A vague anger swelled in her throat. She noticed, too, Roger's silence and Lady Barnes's discomfort. There was clearly something here that had been kept from her—something to be unravelled!

Suddenly the new-comer rose. Mrs. Fairmile wore a dress of some pale gray stuff, cobweb-light and transparent, over a green satin. It had the effect of sea-water, and her gray hat, with its pale green wreath, framed the golden-gray of her hair. Every one of her few adornments was exquisite—so was her grace as she moved. Daphne's pink-and-black vivacity beside her seemed a pinchbeck thing.

"Well, now, when will you all come to Upcott?" Mrs. Fairmile said graciously, as she shook hands. "The Duchess will be enchanted to see you any day, and——"

"Thank you! but we really can't come so far," said a determined voice. "We have only a shaky old motor—our new one isn't ready yet—and besides, we want all our time for the house."

"You make him work so hard?"

Mrs. Fairmile, laughing, pointed to the speaker. Roger looked up involuntarily, and Daphne saw the look.

"Roger has nothing to do," she said, quickly. "Thank you very much: we will certainly come. I'll write to you. How many miles did you say it was?"

"Oh, nothing for a motor!—twenty-five. We used to think it nothing for a ride, didn't we?"

The speaker, who was just passing through the door, turned towards Roger, who with Lelius, was escorting her, with a last gesture—gay, yet, like all her gestures, charged with a slight yet deliberate significance.

They disappeared. Daphne walked to the window, biting her lip.

As she stood there Herbert French came into the room, looking a little shy and ill at ease, and behind him three persons, a clergyman in an Archdeacon's apron and gaiters, and two ladies. Daphne, perceiving them sideways in a mirror to her right, could not repress a gesture and muttered sound of annoyance.

French introduced Archdeacon Mountford, his wife and sister. Roger, it seemed, had met them in the hall, and sent them in. He himself had been carried off on some business by the head keeper.

Daphne turned ungraciously. Her colour was very bright, her eyes a little absent and wild. The two ladies, both clad in pale brown stuffs, large mushroom hats, and stout country boots, eyed her nervously, and as they sat down, at her bidding, they left the Archdeacon—who was the vicar of the neighbouring town—to explain, with much amiable stammering, that seeing the Duchess's carriage at the front door, as they were crossing the park, they presumed that visitors were admitted, and had ventured to call.

Daphne received the explanation without any cordiality. She did indeed bid the callers sit down, and ordered some fresh tea. But she took no pains to entertain them, and if Lady Barnes and Herbert French had not come to the rescue, they would have fared but ill. The Archdeacon, in fact, did come to grief. For him Mrs. Barnes was just a "foreigner," imported from some unknown and, of course, inferior *milieu*, one who had never been "a happy English child," and must therefore be treated with indulgence. He endeavoured to talk to her—kindly—about her country. A branch of his own family, he informed her, had settled about a hundred years before this date in the United States. He gave her, at some length, the genealogy of the branch, then of the main stock to which he himself belonged, presuming that she was, at any rate, acquainted with the name? It was, he said, his strong opinion that American women were very "bright." For himself he could not say that he even disliked the accent, it was so "quaint." Did Mrs. Barnes know many of the American bishops? He himself had met a large number of them at a reception at the Church House, but it had really made him quite uncomfortable! They wore no official dress, and there was he—a mere Archdeacon!—in gaiters. And, of course, no one thought of calling them "my lord." It certainly was very curious—to an Englishman. And Methodist bishops!—such as he was told America possessed in plenty—that was still more curious. One of the Episcopalian bishops, however, had preached—in Westminster Abbey—a remarkable sermon, on a very sad subject, not perhaps a subject to be discussed in a drawing-room—but still——

Suddenly the group on the other side of the room became aware that the Archdeacon's amiable prosing had been sharply interrupted—that Daphne, not he, was holding the field. A gust of talk arose—Daphne declaiming, the Archdeacon, after a first pause of astonishment, changing aspect and tone. French, looking across the room, saw the mask of conventional amiability stripped from what was really a strong and rather tyrannical face. The man's prominent mouth and long upper lip emerged. He drew his chair back from Daphne's; he tried once or twice to stop or argue with her, and finally he rose abruptly.

"My dear!"—his wife turned hastily—"We must not detain Mrs. Barnes longer!"

The two ladies looked at the Archdeacon—the god of their idolatry; then at Daphne. Hurriedly, like birds frightened by a shot, they crossed the room and just touched their hostess's hand; the Archdeacon, making up for their precipitancy by a double dose of dignity, bowed himself out; the door closed behind them.

"Daphne!—my dear! what is the matter?" cried Lady Barnes, in dismay.

"He spoke to me impertinently about my country!" said Daphne, turning upon her, her black eyes blazing, her cheeks white with excitement.

"The Archdeacon!—he is always so polite!"

"He talked like a fool—about things he doesn't understand!" was Daphne's curt reply, as she gathered up her hat and some letters, and moved towards the door.

"About what? My dear Daphne! He could not possibly have meant to offend you! Could he, Mr. French?" Lady Barnes turned plaintively towards her very uncomfortable companions.

Daphne confronted her.

"If he chooses to think America immoral and degraded because American divorce laws are different from the English laws, let him think it!—but he has no business to air his views to an American—at a first visit, too!" said Daphne passionately, and, drawing herself up, she swept out of the room, leaving the others dumfounded.

"Oh dear! oh dear!" wailed Lady Barnes. "And the Archdeacon is so important! Daphne might have been rude to anybody else—but not the Archdeacon!"

"How did they manage to get into such a subject—so quickly?" asked Elsie in bewilderment.

"I suppose he took it for granted that Daphne agreed with him! All decent people do."

Lady Barnes's wrath was evident—so was her indiscretion. Elsie French applied herself to soothing her, while Herbert French disappeared into the garden with a book. His wife, however, presently observed from the drawing-room that he was not reading. He was pacing the lawn, with his hands behind him, and his eyes on the grass. The slight, slowly-moving figure stood for meditation, and Elsie French knew enough to understand that the incidents of the afternoon might well supply any friend of Roger Barnes's with food for meditation. Herbert had not been in the drawing-room when Mrs. Fairmile was calling, but no doubt he had met her in the hall when she was on her way to her carriage.

Meanwhile Daphne, in her own room, was also employed in meditation. She had thrown herself, frowning, into a chair beside a window which overlooked the park. The landscape had a gentle charm—spreading grass, low hills, and scattered woods—under a warm September sun. But it had no particular accent, and Daphne thought it both tame and depressing; like an English society made up of Archdeacon Mountfords and their women-kind! What a futile, irritating man!—and what dull creatures were the wife and daughter!—mere echoes of their lord and master. She had behaved badly, of course; in a few days she supposed the report of her outburst would be all over the place. She did not care. Even for Roger's sake she was not going to cringe to these poor provincial standards.

And all the time she knew very well that it was not the Archdeacon and his fatuities that were really at fault. The afternoon had been decided not by the Mountfords' call, but by that which had preceded it.

CHAPTER VI

Mrs. Barnes, however, made no immediate reference to the matter which was in truth filling her mind. She avoided her husband and mother-in-law, both of whom were clearly anxious to capture her attention; and, by way of protecting herself from them, she spent the late afternoon in looking through Italian photographs with Dr. Lelius.

But about seven o'clock Roger found her lying on her sofa, her hands clasped behind her head—frowning—the lips working.

He came in rather consciously, glancing at his wife in hesitation.

"Are you tired, Daphne?"

"No."

"A penny for your thoughts, then!" He stooped over her and looked into her eyes.

Daphne made no reply. She continued to look straight before her.

"What's the matter with you?" he said, at last.

"I'm wondering," said Daphne slowly, "how many more cousins and great friends you have, that I know nothing about. I think another time it would be civil—just that!—to give me a word of warning."

Roger pulled at his moustache. "I hadn't an idea she was within a thousand miles of this place! But, if I had, I couldn't have imagined she would have the face to come here!"

"Who is she?" With a sudden movement Daphne turned her eyes upon him.

"Well, there's no good making any bones about it," said the man, flushing. "She's a girl I was once engaged to, for a very short time," he added hastily. "It was the week before my father died, and our smash came. As soon as it came she threw me over."

Daphne's intense gaze, under the slightly frowning brows, disquieted him.

"How long were you engaged to her?"

"Three weeks."

"Had she been staying here before that?"

"Yes—she often stayed here. Daphne! don't look like that! She treated me abominably; and before I married you I had come not to care twopence about her."

"You did care about her when you proposed to me?"

"No!—not at all! Of course, when I went out to New York I was sore, because she had thrown me over."

"And I"—Daphne made a scornful lip—"was the feather-bed to catch you as you fell. It never occurred to you that it might have been honourable to tell me?"

"Well, I don't know—I never asked you to tell me of your affairs!"

Roger, his hands in his pockets, looked round at her with an awkward laugh.

"I told you everything!" was the quick reply—"*everything.*"

Roger uncomfortably remembered that so indeed it had been; and moreover that he had been a good deal bored at the time by Daphne's confessions.

He had not been enough in love with her—then—to find them of any great account. And certainly it had never occurred to him to pay them back in kind. What did it matter to her or to anyone that Chloe Morant had made a fool of him? His recollection of the fooling, at the time he proposed to Daphne, was still so poignant that it would have been impossible to speak of it. And within a few months afterwards he had practically forgotten it—and Chloe too. Of course he could not see her again, for the first time, without being "a bit upset"; mostly, indeed, by the boldness—the brazenness—of her behaviour. But his emotions were of no tragic strength, and, as Lady Barnes had complained to Mrs. French, he was now honestly in love with Daphne and his child.

So that he had nothing but impatience and annoyance for the recollection of the visit of the afternoon; and Daphne's attitude distressed him. Why, she was as pale as a ghost! His thoughts sent Chloe Fairmile to the deuce.

"Look here, dear!" he said, kneeling down suddenly beside his wife—"don't you get any nonsense into your head. I'm not the kind of fellow who goes philandering after a woman when she's jilted him. I took her measure, and after you accepted me I never gave her another thought. I forgot her, dear—bag and baggage! Kiss me, Daphne!"

But Daphne still held him at bay.

"How long were you engaged to her?" she repeated.

"I've told you—three weeks!" said the man, reluctantly.

"How long had you known her?"

"A year or two. She was a distant cousin of father's. Her father was Governor of Madras, and her mother was dead. She couldn't stand India for long together, and she used to stay about with relations. Why she took a fancy to me I can't imagine. She's so booky and artistic, and that kind of thing, that I never understood half the time what she was talking about. Now you're just as clever, you know, darling, but I do understand you."

Roger's conscience made a few dim remonstrances. It asked him whether in fact, standing on his own qualifications and advantages of quite a different kind, he had not always felt himself triumphantly more than a match for Chloe and her cleverness. But he paid no heed to them. He was engaged in stroking Daphne's fingers and studying the small set face.

"Whom did she marry?" asked Daphne, putting an end to the stroking.

"A fellow in the army—Major Fairmile—a smart, popular sort of chap. He was her father's aide-de-camp when they married—just after we did—and they've been in India, or Egypt, ever since. They don't get on, and I suppose she comes and quarters herself on the old Duchess—as she used to on us."

"You seem to know all about her! Yes, I remember now, I've heard people speak of her to you. Mrs. Fairmile—Mrs. Fairmile—yes, I remember," said Daphne, in a brooding voice, her cheeks becoming suddenly very red. "Your uncle—in town—mentioned her. I didn't take any notice."

"Why should you? She doesn't matter a fig, either to you or to me!"

"It matters to me very much that these people who spoke of her—your uncle and the others—knew what I didn't know!" cried Daphne, passionately. She stared at Roger, strangely conscious that something epoch-making and decisive had happened. Roger had had a secret from her all these years—that was what had happened; and now she had discovered it. That he *could* have a secret from her, however, was the real discovery. She felt a fierce resentment, and yet a kind of added respect for him. All the time he had been the private owner of thoughts and recollections that she had no part in, and the fact roused in her tumult and bitterness. Nevertheless the disturbance which it produced in her sense of property, the shock and anguish of it, brought back something of the passion of love she had felt in the first year of their marriage.

During these three years she had more than once shown herself insanely jealous for the merest trifles. But Roger had always laughed at her, and she had ended by laughing at herself.

Yet all the time he had had this secret. She sat looking at him hard with her astonishing eyes; and he grew more and more uneasy.

"Well, some of them knew," he said, answering her last reproach. "And they knew that I was jolly well quit of her! I suppose I ought to have told you, Daphne—of course I ought—I'm sorry. But the fact was I never wanted to think of her again. And I certainly never want to see her again! Why, in the name of goodness, did you accept that tea-fight?"

"Because I mean to go."

"Then you'll have to go without me," was the incautious reply.

"Oh, so you're afraid of meeting her! I shall know what to think, if you *don't* go." Daphne sat erect, her hands clasped round her knees.

Roger made a sound of wrath, and threw his cigarette into the fire. Then, turning round again to face her, he tried to control himself.

"Look here, Daphne, don't let us quarrel about this. I'll tell you everything you want to know—the whole beastly story. But it can't be pleasant to me to meet a woman who treated me as she did—and it oughtn't to be pleasant to you either. It was like her audacity to come this afternoon."

"She simply wants to get hold of you again!" Daphne sprang up as she spoke with a violent movement, her face blazing.

"Nonsense! she came out of nothing in the world but curiosity, and because she likes making people uncomfortable. She knew very well mother and I didn't want her!"

But the more he tried to persuade her the more determined was Daphne to pay the promised visit, and that he should pay it with her. He gave way at last, and she allowed herself to be soothed and caressed. Then, when she seemed to have recovered herself, he gave her a tragic-comic account of the three weeks' engagement, and the manner in which it had been broken off: caustic enough, one might have thought, to satisfy the most unfriendly listener. Daphne heard it all quietly.

Then her maid came, and she donned a tea-gown.

When Roger returned, after dressing, he found her still abstracted.

"I suppose you kissed her?" she said abruptly, as they stood by the fire together.

He broke out in laughter and annoyance, and called her a little goose, with his arm round her.

But she persisted. "You did kiss her?"

"Well, of course I did! What else is one engaged for?"

"I'm certain she wished for a great deal of kissing!" said Daphne, quickly.

Roger was silent. Suddenly there swept through him the memory of the scene in the orchard, and with it an admission—wrung, as it were, from a wholly unwilling self—that it had remained for him a scene unique and unapproached. In that one hour the "muddy vesture" of common feeling and desire that closed in his manhood had taken fire and burnt to a pure flame, fusing, so it seemed, body and soul. He had not thought of it for years, but now that he was made to think of it, the old thrill returned—a memory of something heavenly, ecstatic, far transcending the common hours and the common earth.

The next moment he had thrown the recollection angrily from him. Stooping to his wife, he kissed her warmly. "Look here, Daphne! I wish you'd let that woman alone! Have I ever looked at anyone but you, old girl, since that day at Mount Vernon?"

Daphne let him hold her close: but all the time, thoughts—ugly thoughts—like "little mice stole in and out." The notion of Roger and that woman, in the past, engaged—always together, in each other's arms, tormented her unendurably.

She did not, however, say a word to Lady Barnes on the subject. The morning following Mrs. Fairmile's visit that lady began a rather awkward explanation of Chloe Fairmile's place in the family history, and of the reasons for Roger's silence and her own. Daphne took it apparently with complete indifference, and managed to cut it short in the middle.

Nevertheless she brooded over the whole business; and her resentment showed itself, first of all, in a more and more drastic treatment of Heston, its pictures, decorations and appointments. Lady Barnes dared not oppose her any more. She understood that if she were thwarted, or even criticized, Daphne would simply decline to live there, and her own link with the place would be once more broken. So she withdrew angrily from the scene, and tried not to know what was going on. Meanwhile a note of invitation had been addressed to Daphne by the Duchess, and had been accepted; Roger had been reminded, at the point of the bayonet, that go he must; and Dr. Lelius had transferred himself from Heston to Upcott, and the companionship of Mrs. Fairmile.

It was the last day of the Frenches' visit. Roger and Herbert French had been trying to get a brace or two of partridges on the long-neglected and much-poached estate; and on the way home French expressed a hope that, now they were to settle at Heston, Roger would take up some of the usual duties of the country gentleman. He spoke in the half-jesting way characteristic of the modern Mentor. The old didactics have long gone out of fashion, and the moralist of to-day, instead of preaching, *ore retundo*, must only "hint a fault and hesitate dislike." But, hide it as he might, there was an ethical and religious passion in French that would out, and was soon indeed to drive him from Eton to a town parish. He had been ordained some two years before this date.

It was this inborn pastoral gift, just as real as the literary or artistic gifts, and containing the same potentialities of genius as they which was leading him to feel a deep anxiety about the Barnes's *ménage*. It seemed to him necessary that Daphne should respect her husband; and Roger, in a state of complete idleness, was not altogether respectable.

So, with much quizzing of him as "the Squire," French tried to goad his companion into some of a Squire's duties. "Stand for the County Council, old fellow," he said. "Your father was on it, and it'll give you something to do."

To his surprise Roger at once acquiesced. He was striding along in cap and knickerbockers, his curly hair still thick and golden on his temples, his clear skin flushed with exercise, his general physical aspect even more splendid than it had been in his first youth. Beside him, the slender figure and pleasant irregular face of Herbert French would have been altogether effaced and eclipsed but for the Eton master's two striking points: prematurely white hair, remarkably thick and abundant; and very blue eyes, shy, spiritual and charming.

"I don't mind," Roger was saying, "if you think they'd have me. Beastly bore, of course! But one's got to do something for one's keep."

He looked round with a smile, slightly conscious. The position he had occupied for some three years, of the idle and penniless husband dependent on his wife's dollars, was not, he knew, an exalted one in French's eyes.

"Oh! you'll find it quite tolerable," said French. "Roads and schools do as well as anything else to break one's teeth on. We shall see you a magistrate directly."

Roger laughed. "That would be a good one!—I say, you know, I hope Daphne's going to like Heston."

French hoped so too, guardedly.

"I hear the Archdeacon got on her nerves yesterday?"

He looked at his companion with a slight laugh and a shrug.

"That doesn't matter."

"I don't know. He's rather a spiteful old party. And Daphne's accustomed to be made a lot of, you know. In London there's always a heap of people making up to her—and in Paris, too. She talks uncommon good French—learnt it in the convent. I don't understand a word of what they talk about—but she's a queen—I can tell you! She doesn't want Archdeacons prating at her."

"It'll be all right when she knows the people."

"Of course, mother and I get along here all right. We've got to pick up the threads again; but we do know all the people, and we like the old place for grandfather's sake, and all the rest of it. But there isn't much to amuse Daphne here."

"She'll be doing up the house."

"And offending mother all the time. I say, French, don't you think art's an awful nuisance! When I hear Lelius yarning on about *quattro-cento* and *cinque-cento*, I could drown myself. No! I suppose you're tarred with the same brush." Roger shrugged his shoulders. "Well, I don't care, so long as Daphne gets what she wants, and the place suits the child." His ruddy countenance took a shade of anxiety.

French inquired what reason there was to suppose that Beatty would not thrive perfectly at Heston. Roger could only say that the child had seemed to flag a little since their arrival. Appetite not quite so good, temper difficult, and so on. Their smart lady-nurse was not quite satisfied. "And I've been finding out about doctors here," the young father went on, knitting his brows: "blokes, most of them, and such old blokes! I wouldn't trust Beatty to one of them. But I've heard of a new man at Hereford—awfully good, they say—a wunner! And after all a motor would soon run him out!"

He went on talking eagerly about the child, her beauty, her cleverness, the plans Daphne had for her bringing up, and so on. No other child ever had been, ever could be, so fetching, so "cunning," so lovely, such a duck! The Frenches, indeed, possessed a boy of two, reputed handsome. Roger wished to show himself indulgent to anything that might be pleaded for him. "Dear little fellow!"—of course. But Beatty! Well! it was surprising, indeed, that he should find himself the father of such a little miracle; he didn't know what he'd done to deserve it. Herbert French smiled as he walked.

"Of course, I hope there'll be a boy," said Roger, stopping suddenly to look at Heston Park, half a mile off, emerging from the trees. "Daphne would like a boy—so should I, and particularly now that we've got the old house back again."

He stood and surveyed it. French noticed in the growing manliness of his face and bearing the signs of things and forces ancestral, of those ghostly hands stretching from the past that in a long settled society tend to push a man into his right place and keep him there. The Barnes family was tolerable, though not distinguished. Roger's father's great temporary success in politics and business had given it a passing splendour, now quenched in the tides of failure and disaster which had finally overwhelmed his career. Roger evidently did not want to think much about his Barnes heritage. But it was clear also that he was proud of the Trescoes; that he had fallen back upon them, so to speak. Since the fifteenth century there had always been a Trescoe at Heston; and Roger had already taken to browsing in county histories and sorting family letters. French foresaw a double-barrelled surname before long—perhaps, just in time for the advent of the future son and heir who was already a personage in the mind, if not yet positively expected.

"My dear fellow, I hope Mrs. Barnes will give you not one son, but many!" he said, in answer to his companion's outburst. "They're wanted nowadays."

Roger nodded and smiled, and then passed on to discussion of county business and county people. He had already, it seemed, informed himself to a rather surprising degree. The shrewd, upright county gentleman was beginning to emerge, oddly, from the Apollo. The merits and absurdities of the type were already there, indeed, *in posse*. How persistent was the type, and the instinct! A man of Roger's antecedents might seem to swerve from the course; but the smallest favourable variation of circumstances, and there he was again on the track, trotting happily between the shafts.

"If only the wife plays up!" thought French.

The recollection of Daphne, indeed, emerged simultaneously in both minds.

"Daphne, you know, won't be able to stand this all the year round," said Roger. "By George, no! not with a wagon-load of Leliuses!" Then, with a sudden veer and a flush: "I say, French, do you know what sort of state the Fairmile marriage is in by now? I think that lady might have spared her call—don't you?"

French kept his eyes on the path. It was the first time, as far as he was concerned, that Roger had referred to the incident. Yet the tone of the questioner implied a past history. It was to him, indeed, that Roger had come, in the first bitterness of his young grief and anger, after the "jilting." French had tried to help him, only to find that he was no more a match for the lady than the rest of the world.

As to the call and the invitation, he agreed heartily that a person of delicacy would have omitted them. The Fairmile marriage, it was generally rumoured, had broken down hopelessly.

"Faults on both sides, of course. Fairmile is and always was an unscrupulous beggar! He left Eton just as you came, but I remember him well."

Roger began a sentence to the effect that if Fairmile had no scruples of his own, Chloe would scarcely have taught him any; but he checked himself abruptly in the middle, and the two men passed to other topics. French began to talk of East London, and the parish he was to have there. Roger, indifferent at first, did not remain so. He did not profess, indeed, any enthusiasm of humanity; but French found in him new curiosities. That children should starve, and slave, and suffer—*that* moved him. He was, at any rate, for hanging the parents.

The day of the Upcott visit came, and, in spite of all recalcitrance, Roger was made to mount the motor beside his wife. Lady Barnes had entirely refused to go, and Mr. and Mrs. French had departed that morning for Eton.

As the thing was inevitable, Roger's male philosophy came to his aid. Better laugh and have done with it. So that, as he and Daphne sped along the autumn lanes, he talked about anything and everything. He expressed, for instance, his friendly admiration for Elsie French.

"She's just the wife for old Herbert—and, by George, she's in love with him!"

"A great deal too much in love with him!" said Daphne, sharply. The day was chilly, with a strong east wind blowing, and Daphne's small figure and face were enveloped in a marvellous wrap, compounded in equal proportions of Russian sables and white cloth. It had not long arrived from Wörth, and Roger had allowed himself some jibes as to its probable cost. Daphne's "simplicity," the pose of her girlhood, was in fact breaking down in all directions. The arrogant spending instinct had gained upon the moderating and self-restraining instinct. The results often made Barnes uncomfortable. But he was inarticulate, and easily intimidated—by Daphne. With regard to Mrs. French, however, he took up the cudgels at once. Why shouldn't Elsie adore her man, if it pleased her? Old Herbert was worth it.

Women, said Daphne, should never put themselves wholly in a man's power. Moreover, wifely adoration was particularly bad for clergymen, who were far too much inclined already to give themselves airs.

"I say! Herbert never gives himself airs!"

"They both did—to me. They have quite different ways from us, and they make one feel it. They have family prayers—we don't. They have ascetic ideas about bringing up children—I haven't. Elsie would think it self-indulgent and abominable to stay in bed to breakfast—I don't. The fact is, all her interests and ideals are quite different from mine, and I am rather tired of being made to feel inferior."

"Daphne! what rubbish! I'm certain Elsie French never had such an idea in her head. She's awfully soft and nice; I never saw a bit of conceit in her."

"She's soft outside and steel inside. Well, never mind! we don't get on. She's the old America, I'm the new," said Daphne, half frowning, half laughing; "and I'm as good as she."

"You're a very good-looking woman, anyway," said Roger, admiring the vision of her among the warm browns and shining whites of her wrap. "Much better-looking than when I married you." He slipped an arm under the cloak and gave her small waist a squeeze.

Daphne turned her eyes upon him. In their black depths his touch had roused a passion which was by no means all tenderness. There was in it something threatening, something intensely and inordinately possessive. "That means that you didn't think me good-looking at all, as compared with—Chloe?" she said insistently.

"Really, Daphne!"—Roger withdrew his arm with a rather angry laugh—"the way you twist what one says! I declare I won't make you any more pretty speeches for an age."

Daphne scarcely replied; but there dawned on her face the smile—melting, provocative, intent—which is the natural weapon of such a temperament. With a quick movement she nestled to her husband's side, and Roger was soon appeased.

The visit which followed always counted in Roger Barnes's memory as the first act of the tragedy, the first onset of the evil that engulfed him.

They found the old Duchess, Mrs. Fairmile, and Dr. Lelius, alone. The Duchess had been the penniless daughter of an Irish clergyman, married *en secondes noces* for her somewhat queer and stimulating personality, by an epicurean duke, who, after having provided the family with a sufficient store of dull children by an aristocratic mother, thought himself at liberty, in his declining years, to please himself. He had left her the dower-house—small but delicately Jacobean—and she was now nearly as old as the Duke had been when he married her. She was largely made, shapeless, and untidy. Her mannish face and head were tied up in a kind of lace coif; she had long since abandoned all thought of a waist; and her strong chin rested on an ample bosom.

As soon as Mrs. Barnes was seated near her hostess, Lelius—who had an intimate acquaintance, through their pictures, with half the great people of Europe—began to observe the Duchess's impressions. Amused curiosity, first. Evidently Daphne represented to her one of the queer, crude types that modern society is always throwing up on the shores of life—like strange beasts from deep-sea soundings.

An American heiress, half Spanish—South-American Spanish—with no doubt a dash of Indian; no manners, as Europe understands them; unlimited money, and absurd pretensions—so Chloe said—in the matter of art; a mixture of the pedant and the *parvenue*; where on earth had young Barnes picked her up! It was in some such way, no doubt—so Lelius guessed—that the Duchess's thoughts were running.

Meanwhile Mrs. Barnes was treated with all possible civility. The Duchess inquired into the plans for rebuilding Heston; talked of her own recollections of the place, and its owners; hoped that Mrs. Barnes was pleased with the neighbourhood; and finally asked the stock question, "And how do you like England?"

Daphne looked at her coolly. "Moderately!" she said, with a smile, the colour rising in her cheek as she became aware, without looking at them, that Roger and Mrs. Fairmile had adjourned to the farther end of the large room, leaving her to the Duchess and Lelius.

The small eyes above the Duchess's prominent nose sparkled. "Only moderately?" The speaker's tone expressed that she had been for once taken by surprise. "I'm extremely sorry we don't please you, Mrs. Barnes."

"You see, my expectations were so high."

"Is it the country, or the climate, or the people, that won't do?" inquired the Duchess, amused.

"I suppose it would be civil to say the climate," replied Daphne, laughing.

Whereupon the Duchess saw that her visitor had made up her mind not to be overawed. The great lady summoned Dr. Lelius to her aid, and she, the German, and Daphne, kept up a sparring conversation, in which Mrs. Barnes, driven on by a secret wrath, showed herself rather noisier than Englishwomen generally are. She was a little impertinent, the Duchess thought, decidedly aggressive, and not witty enough to carry it off.

Meanwhile, Daphne had instantly perceived that Mrs. Fairmile and Roger had disappeared into the conservatory; and though she talked incessantly through their absence, she felt each minute of it. When they came back for tea, she imagined that Roger looked embarrassed, while Mrs. Fairmile was all gaiety, chatting to her companion, her face raised to his, in the manner of one joyously renewing an old intimacy. As they slowly advanced up the long room, Daphne felt it almost intolerable to watch them, and her pulses began to race. *Why* had she never been told of this thing? That was what rankled; and the Southern wildness in her blood sent visions of the past and terrors of the future hurrying through her brain, even while she went on talking fast and recklessly to the Duchess.

At tea-time conversation turned on the various beautiful things which the room contained—its Nattiers, its Gobelins, its two *dessus de portes* by Boucher, and its two cabinets, of which one had belonged to Beaumarchais and the other to the *Appartement du Dauphin* at Versailles.

Daphne restrained herself for a time, asked questions, and affected no special knowledge. Then, at a pause, she lifted a careless hand, inquiring whether "the Fragonard sketch" opposite were not the pendant of one—she named it—at Berlin.

"Ah-h-h!" said Mrs. Fairmile, with a smiling shake of the head, "how clever of you! But that's not a Fragonard. I wish it were. It's an unknown. Dr. Lelius has given him a name."

And she and Lelius fell into a discussion of the drawing, that soon left Daphne behind. Native taste of the finest, mingled with the training of a lifetime, the intimate knowledge of collections of one who had lived among them from her childhood—these things had long since given Chloe Fairmile a kind of European reputation. Daphne stumbled after her, consumed with angry envy, the *précieuse* in her resenting the easy mastery of Mrs. Fairmile, and the wife in her offended by the strange beauty, the soft audacities of a woman who had once, it seemed, held Roger captive, and would, of course, like to hold him captive again.

She burned in some way to assert herself, the imperious will chafing at the slender barrier of self-control. And some malicious god did, in fact, send an opportunity.

After tea, when Roger, in spite of efforts to confine himself to the Duchess, had been once more drawn into the orbit of Mrs. Fairmile, as she sat fingering a cigarette between the two men, and gossiping of people and politics, the butler entered, and whispered a message to the Duchess.

The mistress of the house laughed. "Chloe! who do you think has called? Old Marcus, of South Audley Street. He's been at Brendon House—buying up their Romneys, I should think. And as he was passing here, he wished to show me something. Shall we have him in?"

"By all means! The last time he was here he offered you four thousand pounds for the blue Nattier," said Chloe, with a smile, pointing to the picture.

The Duchess gave orders; and an elderly man, with long black hair, swarthy complexion, fine eyes, and a peaked forehead, was admitted, and greeted by her, Mrs. Fairmile, and Dr. Lelius as an old acquaintance. He sat down beside them, was given tea, and presented to Mr. and Mrs. Barnes. Daphne, who knew the famous dealer by sight and reputation perfectly well, was piqued that he did not recognize her. Yet she well remembered having given him an important commission not more than a year before her marriage.

As soon as a cup of tea had been dispatched, Marcus came to the business. He drew a small leather case out of the bag he had brought into the room with him; and the case, being opened, disclosed a small but marvellous piece of Sèvres.

"There!" he said, pointing triumphantly to a piece on the Duchess's chimney-piece. "Your Grace asked me—oh! ten years ago—and again last year—to find you the pair of that. Now—you have it!"

He put the two together, and the effect was great. The Duchess looked at it with greed—the greed of the connoisseur. But she shook her head.

"Marcus, I have no money."

"Oh!" He protested, smiling and shrugging his shoulders.

"And I know you want a brigand's price for it."

"Oh, nothing—nothing at all."

The Duchess took it up, and regretfully turned it round and round.

"A thousand, Marcus?" she said, looking up.

He laughed, and would not reply.

"That means more, Marcus: how do you imagine that an old woman like me, with only just enough for bread and butter, can waste her money on Sèvres?" He grinned. She put it down resolutely. "No! I've got a consumptive nephew with a consumptive family. He ought to have been hung for marrying, but I've got to send them all to Davos this winter. No, I can't, Marcus; I can't—I'm too poor." But her eyes caressed the shining thing.

Daphne bent forward. "If the Duchess has *really* made up her mind, Mr. Marcus, I will take it. It would just suit me!"

Marcus started on his chair. "*Pardon, Madame!*" he said, turning hastily to look at the slender lady in white, of whom he had as yet taken no notice.

"We have the motor. We can take it with us," said Daphne, stretching out her hand for it triumphantly.

"Madame," said Marcus, in some agitation, "I have not the honour. The price——"

"The price doesn't matter," said Daphne, smiling. "You know me quite well, Mr. Marcus. Do you remember selling a Louis Seize cabinet to Miss Floyd?"

"Ah!" The dealer was on his feet in a moment, saluting, excusing himself. Daphne heard him with graciousness. She was now the centre of the situation: she had asserted herself, and her money. Marcus outdid himself in homage. Lelius in the background looked on, a sarcastic smile hidden by his fair moustache. Mrs. Fairmile, too, smiled; Roger had grown rather hot; and the Duchess was frankly annoyed.

"I surrender it to *force majeure*," she said, as Daphne took it from her. "Why are we not all Americans?"

And then, leaning back in her chair, she would talk no more. The pleasure of the visit, so far as it had ever existed, was at an end.

But before the Barnes motor departed homewards, Mrs. Fairmile had again found means to carry Roger Barnes out of sight and hearing into the garden. Roger had not been able to avoid it; and Daphne, hugging the leather case, had, all the same, to look on.

When they were once more alone together, speeding through the bright sunset air, each found the other on edge.

"You were rather rough on the Duchess, Daphne!" Roger protested. "It wasn't quite nice, was it, outbidding her like that in her own house?"

Daphne flared up at once, declaring that she wanted no lessons in deportment from him or anyone else, and then demanding fiercely what was the meaning of his two disappearances with Mrs. Fairmile. Whereupon Roger lost his temper still more decidedly, refusing to give any account of himself, and the drive passed in a continuous quarrel, which only just stopped short, on Daphne's side, of those outrageous and insulting things which were burning at the back of her tongue, while she could not as yet bring herself to say them.

An unsatisfactory peace was patched up during the evening. But in the dead of night Daphne sat up in bed, looking at the face and head of her husband beside her on the pillow. He lay peacefully sleeping, the noble outline of brow and features still nobler in the dim light which effaced all the weaker, emptier touches. Daphne felt rising within her that mingled passion of the jealous woman, which is half love, half hate, of which she had felt the first stirrings in her early jealousy of Elsie Maddison. It was the clutch of something racial and inherited—a something which the Northerner hardly knows. She had felt it before on one or two occasions, but not with this intensity. The grace of Chloe Fairmile haunted her memory, and the perfection, the corrupt perfection of her appeal to men, men like Roger.

"In the dead of night Daphne sat up in bed, looking at the face and head of her husband beside her on the pillow."

She must wring from him—she must and would—a much fuller history of his engagement. And of those conversations in the garden, too. It stung her to recollect that, after all, he had given her no account of them. She had been sure they had not been ordinary conversations!—Mrs. Fairmile was not the person to waste her time in chit-chat.

A gust of violence swept through her. She had given Roger everything—money, ease, amusement. Where would he have been without her? And his mother, too?—tiresome, obstructive woman! For the first time that veil of the unspoken, that mist of loving illusion which preserves all human relations, broke down between Daphne and her marriage. Her thoughts dwelt, in a vulgar detail, on the money she had settled upon

Roger—on his tendencies to extravagance—his happy-go-lucky self-confident ways. He would have been a pauper but for her; but now that he had her money safe, without a word to her of his previous engagement, he and Mrs. Fairmile might do as they pleased. The heat and corrosion of this idea spread through her being, and the will made no fight against it.

CHAPTER VII

"You're off to the meet?"

"I am. Look at the day!"

Chloe Fairmile, who was standing in her riding-habit at the window of the Duchess's morning-room, turned to greet her hostess.

A mild November sun shone on the garden and the woods, and Chloe's face—the more exquisite as a rule for its slight, strange withering—had caught a freshness from the morning.

The Duchess was embraced, and bore it; she herself never kissed anybody.

"You always look well, my dear, in a habit, and you know it. Tell me what I shall do with this invitation."

"From Lady Warton? May I look?"

Chloe took a much blotted and crossed letter from the Duchess's hand.

"What were her governesses about?" said the Duchess, pointing to it. "*Really*—the education of our class! Read it!"

... "Can I persuade you to come—and bring Mrs. Fairmile—next Tuesday to dinner, to meet Roger Barnes and his wife? I groan at the thought, for I think she is quite one of the most disagreeable little creatures I ever saw. But Warton says I must—a Lord-Lieutenant can't pick and choose!—and people as rich as they are have to be considered. I can't imagine why it is she makes herself so odious. All the Americans I ever knew I have liked particularly. It is, of course, annoying that they have so much money—but Warton says it isn't their fault—it's Protection, or something of the kind. But Mrs. Barnes seems really to wish to trample on us. She told Warton the other day that his tapestries—you know, those we're so proud of—that they were bad Flemish copies of something or other—a set belonging to a horrid friend of hers, I think. Warton was furious. And she's made the people at Brendon love her for ever by insisting that they have now ruined all their pictures without exception, by the way they've had them restored—et cetera, et cetera. She really makes us feel her millions—and her brains—too much. We're paupers, but we're not worms. Then there's the Archdeacon—why should she fall foul of him? He tells Warton that her principles are really shocking. She told him she saw no reason why people should stick to their husbands or wives longer than it pleased them—and that in America nobody did! He doesn't wish Mrs. Mountford to see much of her;—though, really, my dear, I don't think Mrs. M. is likely to give him trouble—do you? And I hear, of course, that she thinks us all dull and stuck-up, and as ignorant as savages. It's so odd she shouldn't even want to be liked!—a young woman in a strange neighbourhood. But she evidently doesn't, a bit. Warton declares she's already tired of Roger—and she's certainly not nice to him. What can be the matter? Anyway, dear Duchess, *do* come, and help us through."

"What, indeed, can be the matter?" repeated Chloe lightly, as she handed back the letter.

"Angela Warton never knows anything. But there's not much need for *you* to ask, my dear," said the Duchess quietly.

Mrs. Fairmile turned an astonished face.

"Me?"

The Duchess, more bulky, shapeless and swathed than usual, subsided on a chair, and just raised her small but sharp eyes on Mrs. Fairmile.

"What can you mean?" said Chloe, after a moment, in her gayest voice. "I can't imagine. And I don't think I'll try."

She stooped and kissed the untidy lady in the chair. The Duchess bore it again, but the lines of her mouth, with the strong droop at the corners, became a trifle grim. Chloe looked at her, smiled, shook her head. The Duchess shook hers, and then they both began to talk of an engagement announced that morning in the *Times*.

Mrs. Fairmile was soon riding alone, without a groom—she was an excellent horsewoman, and she never gave any unnecessary trouble to her friends' servants—through country lanes chequered with pale sun. As for the Duchess's attack upon her, Chloe smarted. The Duchess had clearly pulled her up, and Chloe was not a person who took it well.

If Roger's American wife was by now wildly jealous of his old *fiancée*, whose fault was it? Had not Mrs. Barnes herself thrown them perpetually together? Dinners at Upcott!—invitations to Heston!—a resolute frequenting of the same festal gatherings with Mrs. Fairmile. None of it with Roger's goodwill, or his mother's,—Chloe admitted it. It had been the wife's doing—all of it. There had been even—rare occurrences—two or three balls in the neighbourhood. Roger hated dancing, but Daphne had made him go to them all. Merely that she might display her eyes, her diamonds, and her gowns? Not at all. The real psychology of it was plain. "She wishes to keep us under observation—to give us opportunities—and then torment her husband. Very well then!—*tu l'as voulu, Madame!*"

As to the "opportunities," Chloe coolly confessed to herself that she had made rather a scandalous use of them. The gossip of the neighbourhood had been no doubt a good deal roused; and Daphne, it seemed, was discontented. But is it not good for such people to be discontented? The money and the arrogance of Roger's wife had provoked Roger's former *fiancée* from the beginning; the money to envy, and the arrogance to chastisement. Why not? What is society but a discipline?

As for Roger, who is it says there is a little polygamy in all men? Anyway, a man can always—nearly always—keep a corner for the old love, if the new love will let him. Roger could, at any rate; "though he is a model husband, far better than she deserves, and anybody not a fool could manage him."

It was a day of physical delight, especially for riders. After a warm October, the leaves were still thick on the trees; Nature had not yet resigned herself to death and sleep. Here and there an oak stood, fully green, among the tawny reds and golds of a flaming woodland. The gorse was yellow on the commons; and in the damp woody ways through which Chloe passed, a few primroses—frail, unseasonable blooms—pushed their pale heads through the moss. The scent of the beech-leaves under foot; the buffeting of a westerly wind; the pleasant yielding of her light frame to the movement of the horse; the glimpses of plain that every here and there showed themselves through the trees that girdled the high ground or edge along which she rode; the white steam-wreath of a train passing, far away, through strata of blue or pearly mist; an old windmill black in the middle distance; villages, sheltering among their hedges and uplands: a sky, of shadow below widely brooding over earth, and of a radiant blue flecked with white cloud above:—all the English familiar scene, awoke in Chloe Fairmile a familiar sensuous joy. Life was so good—every minute, every ounce of it! from the Duchess's *chef* to these ethereal splendours of autumn—from the warm bath, the luxurious bed, and breakfast, she had but lately enjoyed, to these artistic memories that ran through her brain, as she glanced from side to side, reminded now of Turner, now of DeWint, revelling in the complexity of her own being. Her conscience gave her no trouble; it had never been more friendly. Her husband and she had come to an understanding; they were in truth more than quits. There was to be no divorce—and no scandal. She would be very prudent. A man's face rose before her that was not the face of her husband, and she smiled—indulgently. Yes, life would be interesting when she returned to town. She had taken a house in Chester Square from the New Year; and Tom was going to Teheran. Meanwhile, she was passing the time.

A thought suddenly occurred to her. Yes, it was quite possible—probable even—that she might find Roger at the meet! The place appointed was a long way from Heston, but in the old days he had often sent on a fresh horse by train to a local station. They had had many a run together over the fields now coming into sight. Though certainly if he imagined there were the very smallest chance of finding her there, he would give this particular meet a wide berth.

Chloe laughed aloud. His resistance—and his weakness—were both so amusing. She thought of the skill—the peremptory smiling skill—with which she had beguiled him into the garden, on the day when the young couple paid their first call at Upcott. First, the low-spoken words at the back of the drawing-room, while Mrs. Barnes and the Duchess were skirmishing—

"I *must* speak to you. Something that concerns another person—something urgent."

Whereupon, unwilling and rather stern compliance on the man's part—the handsome face darkened with most unnecessary frowns. And in the garden, the short colloquy between them—"Of course, I see—you haven't forgiven me! Never mind! I am doing this for someone else—it's a duty." Then abruptly—"You still have three of my letters."

Amusing again—his shock of surprise, his blundering denials! He always was the most unmethodical and unbusiness-like of mortals—poor Roger! She heard her own voice in reply. "Oh yes, you have. I don't make mistakes about such things. Do you remember the letter in which I told you about that affair of Theresa Weightman?"

A stare—an astonished admission. Precisely!

"Well, she's in great trouble. Her husband threatens absurdities. She has always confided in me—she trusts me, and I can't have that letter wandering about the world."

"I certainly sent it back!"

"No—you never sent it back. You have three of mine. And you know how careless you are—how you leave things about. I was always on tenterhooks. Look again, *please*! You must have some idea where they might be."

Perplexity—annoyance!

"When we sold the London house, all papers and documents were sent down here. We reserved a room—which was locked up."

"*A la bonne heure!* Of course—there they are."

But all the same—great unwillingness to search. It was most unlikely he would be able to find anything—most unlikely there was anything to find. He was sure he had sent back everything. And then a look in the fine hazel eyes—like a horse putting back its ears.

All of no avail—against the laughing persistence which insisted on the letters. "But I must have them—I really must! It is a horrid tragedy, and I told you everything—things I had no business to tell you at all."

On which, at last, a grudging consent to look, followed by a marked determination to go back to the drawing-room....

But it was the second *tête-à-tête* that was really adroit! After tea—just a touch on the arm—while the Duchess was showing the Nattiers to Mrs. Barnes, and Lelius was holding the lamp. "One moment more!—in the conservatory. I have a few things to add." And in that second little interview—about nothing, in truth—a mere piece of audacity—the lion's claws had been a good deal pared. He had been made to look at her, first and foremost; to realize that she was not afraid of him—not one bit!—and that he would have to treat her decently. Poor Roger! In a few years the girl he had married would be a plain and prickly little pedant—ill-bred besides—and he knew it.

As to more recent adventures. If people meet in society, they must be civil; and if old friends meet at a dance, there is an institution known as "sitting out"; and "sitting out" is nothing if not conversational; and conversation—between old friends and cousins—is beguiling, and may be lengthy.

The ball at Brendon House—Chloe still felt the triumph of it in her veins—still saw the softening in Roger's handsome face, the look of lazy pleasure, and the disapproval—or was it the envy?—in the eyes of certain county magnates looking on. Since then, no communication between Heston and Upcott.

Mrs. Fairmile was now a couple of miles from the meet. She had struck into a great belt of plantations bounding one side of the ducal estate. Through it ran a famous green ride, crossed near its beginning by a main road. On her right, beyond the thick screen of trees, was the railway, and she could hear the occasional rush of a train.

When she reached the cross road, which led from a station, a labourer opened the plantation gates for her. As he unlatched the second, she perceived a man's figure in front of her.

"Roger!"

A touch of the whip—her horse sprang forward. The man in front looked back startled; but she was already beside him.

"You keep up the old habit, like me? What a lovely day!"

Roger Barnes, after a flush of amazement and surprise, greeted her coldly: "It is a long way for you to come," he said formally. "Twelve miles, isn't it? You're not going to hunt?"

"Oh, no! I only came to look at the hounds and the horses—to remind myself of all the good old times. You don't want to remember them, I know. Life's gone on for you!"

Roger bent forward to pat the neck of his horse. "It goes on for all of us," he said gruffly.

"Ah, well!" She sighed. He looked up and their eyes met. The wind had slightly reddened her pale skin: her expression was one of great animation, yet of great softness. The grace of the long, slender body in the close-fitting habit; of the beautiful head and loosened hair under the small, low-crowned beaver hat; the slender hand upon the reins—all these various impressions rushed upon Barnes at once, bringing with them the fascination of a past happiness, provoking, by contrast, the memory of a harassing and irritating present.

"Is Heston getting on?" asked Mrs. Fairmile, smiling.

He frowned involuntarily.

"Oh, I suppose we shall be straight some day;" the tone, however, belied the words. "When once the British workman gets in, it's the deuce to get him out."

"The old house had such a charm!" said Chloe softly.

Roger made no reply. He rode stiffly beside her, looking straight before him. Chloe, observing him without appearing to do anything of the kind, asked herself whether the Apollo radiance of him were not already somewhat quenched and shorn. A slight thickening of feature—a slight coarsening of form—she thought she perceived them. Poor Roger!—had he been living too well and idling too flagrantly on these American dollars?

Suddenly she bent over and laid a gloved hand on his arm.

"Hadn't it?" she said, in a low voice.

He started. But he neither looked at her nor shook her off.

"What—the house?" was the ungracious reply. "I'm sure I don't know; I never thought about it—whether it was pretty or ugly, I mean. It suited us, and it amused mother to fiddle about with it."

Mrs. Fairmile withdrew her hand.

"Of course a great deal of it was ugly," she said composedly. "Dear Lady Barnes really didn't know. But then we led such a jolly life in it—*we* made it!"

She looked at him brightly, only to see in him an angry flash of expression. He turned and faced her.

"I'm glad you think it was jolly. My remembrances are not quite so pleasant."

She laughed a little—not flinching at all—her face rosy to his challenge.

"Oh, yes, they are—or should be. What's the use of blackening the past because it couldn't be the present. My dear Roger, if I hadn't—well, let's talk plainly!—if I hadn't thrown you over, where would you be now? We should be living in West Kensington, and I should be taking boarders—or—no!—a country-house, perhaps, with paying guests. You would be teaching the cockney idea how to shoot, at half a guinea a day, and I should be buying my clothes second-hand through the *Exchange and Mart*. Whereas—whereas——"

She bent forward again.

"You are a very rich man—you have a charming wife—a dear little girl—you can get into Parliament—travel, speculate, race, anything you please. And I did it all!"

"I don't agree with you," he said drily. She laughed again.

"Well, we can't argue it—can we? I only wanted to point out to you the plain, bare truth, that there is nothing in the world to prevent our being excellent friends again—*now*. But first—and once more—*my letters!*"

Her tone was a little peremptory, and Roger's face clouded.

"I found two of them last night, by the merest chance—in an old dispatch-box I took to America. They were posted to you on the way here."

"Good! But there were three."

"I know—so you said. I could only find two."

"Was the particular letter I mentioned one of them?"

He answered unwillingly.

"No. I searched everywhere. I don't believe I have it."

She shook her head with decision.

"You certainly have it. Please look again."

He broke out with some irritation, insisting that if it had not been returned it had been either lost or destroyed. It could matter to no one.

Some snaring, entangling instinct—an instinct of the hunter—made her persist. She must have it. It was a point of honour. "Poor Theresa is so unhappy, so pursued! You saw that odious paragraph last week? I can't run the risk!"

With a groan of annoyance, he promised at last that he would look again. Then the sparkling eyes changed, the voice softened.

She praised—she rewarded him. By smooth transitions she slipped into ordinary talk; of his candidature for the County Council—the points of the great horse he rode—the gossip of the neighbourhood—the charms of Beatty.

And on this last topic he, too, suddenly found his tongue. The cloud—of awkwardness, or of something else not to be analyzed—broke away, and he began to talk, and presently to ask questions, with readiness, even with eagerness.

Was it right to be so very strict with children?—babies under three? Wasn't it ridiculous to expect them not to be naughty or greedy? Why, every child wanted as much sweetstuff as it could tuck in! Quite right too—doctors said it was good for them. But Miss Farmer——

"Who is Miss Farmer?" inquired Mrs. Fairmile. She was riding close beside him—an embodied friendliness—a soft and womanly Chloe, very different from the old.

"She's the nurse; my mother found her. She's a lady—by way of—she doesn't do any rough work—and I dare say she's the newest thing out. But she's too tight a hand for my taste. I say!—what do you think of this! She wouldn't let Beattie come down to the drawing-room yesterday, because she cried for a sweet! Wasn't that *devilish*!" He brought his hand down fiercely on his thigh.

"A Gorgon!" said Mrs. Fairmile, raising her eyebrows. "Any other qualifications? French? German?"

"Not a word. Not she! Her people live somewhere near here, I believe." Roger looked vaguely round him. "Her father managed a brick-field on this estate—some parson or other recommended her to mother."

"And you don't like her?"

"Well, no—I don't! She's not the kind of woman *I* want." He blurted it out, adding hurriedly, "But my wife thinks a lot of her."

Chloe dismissed the topic of the nurse, but still let him run on about the child. Amazing!—this development of paternity in the careless, handsome youth of three years before. She was amused and bored by it. But her permission of it had thawed him—that she saw.

Presently, from the child she led him on to common acquaintance—old friends—and talk flowed fast. She made him laugh; and the furrows in the young brow disappeared. Now as always they understood each other at a word; there was between them the freemasonry of persons sprung from the same world and the same tradition; his daily talk with Daphne had never this easy, slipping pleasure. Meanwhile the horses sauntered on, unconsciously held back; and the magical autumn wood, its lights and lines and odours, played upon their senses.

At last Roger with a start perceived a gate in front. He looked at his watch, and she saw him redden.

"We shall be late for the meet."

His eyes avoided hers. He gathered up the reins, evidently conscious.

Smiling, she let him open the gate for her, and then as they passed into the road, shadowed with over-arching trees, she reined in Whitefoot, and bending forward, held out her hand. "Good-bye!"

"You're not coming?"

"I think I've had enough. I'll go home. Good-bye."

It was a relief. In both minds had risen the image of their arrival together—amid the crowd of the meet. As he looked at her—gratefully—the grace of her movement, the temptation of her eyes, the rush of old memories suddenly turned his head. He gripped her hand hard for a minute, staring at her.

The road in front of them was quite empty. But fifty yards behind them was a small red-brick house buried in trees. As they still paused, hand in hand, in front of the gate into the wood, which had failed to swing back and remained half open, the garden door of this house unclosed and a young woman in a kind of uniform stepped into the road. She perceived the two riders—stopped in astonishment—observed them unseen, and walked quickly away in the direction of the station.

Roger reached Heston that night only just in time to dress for dinner.

By this time he was in a wholly different mood; angry with himself, and full of rueful thought about his wife. Daphne and he had been getting on anything but well for some time past. He knew that he had several times behaved badly; why, indeed, that very afternoon, had he held Chloe Fairmile's hand in the public road, like an idiot? Suppose anyone had passed? It was only Daphne's tempers and the discomfort at home that made an hour with Chloe so pleasant—and brought the old recollections back. He vowed he never thought of her, except when she was there to make a fool of him—or plague him about those beastly letters. Whereas Daphne—Daphne was always in his mind, and this eclipse into which their daily life had passed. He seemed to be always tripping and stumbling, like a lame man among loose stones; doing or saying what he did not mean to do or say, and tongue-tied when he should have spoken. Daphne's jealousy made him ridiculous; he resented it hotly; yet he knew he was not altogether blameless.

If only something could be done to make Daphne like Heston and the neighbours! But he saw plainly enough that in spite of all the effort and money she was pouring out upon the house, it gave her very little pleasure in return. Her heart was not in it. And as for the neighbours, she had scarcely a good word now for any of them. Jolly!—just as he was going to stand for the County Council, with an idea of Parliament later on! And as for what *he* wished—what would be good for *him*—that she never seemed to think of. And, really, some of the things she said now and then about money—nobody with the spirit of a mouse could stand them.

To comfort his worries he went first of all to the nursery, where he found the nursery-maid in charge, and the child already asleep. Miss Farmer, it appeared, had been enjoying a "day off," and was not expected back till late. He knelt down beside the little girl, feeding his eyes upon her. She lay with her delicate face pressed into the pillow, the small neck visible under the cloud of hair, one hand, the soft palm uppermost, on the sheet. He bent down and kissed the hand, glad that the sharp-faced nurse was not there to see. The touch of the fragrant skin thrilled him with pride and joy; so did the lovely defencelessness of the child's sleep. That such a possession should have been given to him, to guard and cherish! There was in his mind a passionate vow to guard the little thing—aye, with his life-blood; and then a movement of laughter at his own heroics. Well!—Daphne might give him sons—but he did not suppose any other child could ever be quite the same to him as Beatty. He sat in a contented silence, feeding his eyes upon her, as the soft breath rose and fell. And as he did so, his temper softened and warmed toward Beatty's mother.

A little later he found Daphne in her room, already dressed for dinner. He approached her uneasily.

"How tired you look, Daphne! What have you been doing to yourself?"

Daphne stiffly pointed out that she had been standing over the workmen all day, there being no one else to stand over them, and of course she was tired. Her manner would have provoked him but for the visiting of an inward compunction. Instead of showing annoyance he bent down and kissed her.

"I'll stay and help to-morrow, if you want me, though you know I'm no good. I say, how much more are you going to do to the house?"

Daphne looked at him coldly. She had not returned the kiss. "Of course, I know that you don't appreciate in the least what I am doing!"

Roger thrust his hands into his pockets, and walked up and down uncomfortably. He thought, in fact, that Daphne was spoiling the dear nondescript old place, and he knew that the neighbourhood thought so too. Also he particularly disliked the young architect who was superintending the works ("a priggish ass," who gave himself abominable airs—except to Daphne, whom he slavishly obeyed, and to Miss Farmer, with whom Roger had twice caught him gossipping). But he was determined not to anger his wife, and he held his tongue.

"I wish, anyway, you wouldn't stick at it so closely," he said discontentedly. "Let's go abroad somewhere for Christmas—Nice, or Monte Carlo. I am sure you want a change."

"Well, it isn't exactly an enchanting neighbourhood," said Daphne, with pinched lips.

"I'm awfully sorry you don't like the people here," said Roger, perplexed. "I dare say they're all stupids."

"That wouldn't matter—if they behaved decently," said Daphne, flushing.

"I suppose that means—if I behaved decently!" cried Roger, turning upon her.

Daphne faced him, her head in air, her small foot beating the ground, in a trick it had.

"Well, I'm not likely to forget the Brendon ball, am I?"

Roger's look changed.

"I meant no harm, and you know I didn't," he said sulkily.

"Oh, no, you only made a laughing-stock of *me*!" Daphne turned on her heel. Suddenly she felt herself roughly caught in Roger's arms.

"Daphne, what *is* the matter? Why can't we be happy together?"

"Ask yourself," she said, trying to extricate herself, and not succeeding. "I don't like the people here, and they don't like me. But as you seem to enjoy flirting with Mrs. Fairmile, there's one person satisfied."

Roger laughed—not agreeably. "I shall soon think, Daphne, that somebody's 'put a spell on you,' as my old nurse used to say. I wish I knew what I could do to break it."

She lay passive in his arms a moment, and then he felt a shiver run through her, and saw that she was crying. He held her close to him, kissing and comforting her, while his own eyes were wet. What her emotion meant, or his own, he could not have told clearly; but it was a moment for both of healing, of impulsive return, the one to the other, unspoken penitence on her side, a hidden self-blame on his. She clung to him fiercely, courting the pressure of his arms, the warm contact of his youth; while, in his inner mind, he renounced with energy the temptress Chloe and all her works, vowing to himself that he would give Daphne no cause, no pretext even, for jealousy, and would bear it patiently if she were still unjust and tormenting.

"Where have you been all day?" said Daphne at last, disengaging herself, and brushing the tears away from her eyes—a little angrily, as though she were ashamed of them.

"I told you this morning. I had a run with the Stoneshire hounds."

"Whom did you meet there?"

"Oh, various old acquaintances. Nobody amusing." He gave two or three names, his conscience pricking him. Somehow, at that moment, it seemed impossible to mention Chloe Fairmile.

About eleven o'clock that night, Daphne and Lady Barnes having just gone upstairs, Roger and a local Colonel of Volunteers who was dining and spending the night at Heston, were in the smoking-room. Colonel Williams had come over to discuss Volunteer prospects in the neighbourhood, and had been delighted to find in the grandson of his old friend, Oliver Trescoe,—a young fellow whom he and others had too readily regarded as given over to luxury and soft living—signs of the old public spirit, the traditional manliness of the family. The two men were talking with great cordiality, when the sound of a dogcart driving up to the front door disturbed them.

"Who on earth?—at this time of night?" said Roger.

The butler, entering with fresh cigarettes, explained that Miss Farmer had only just returned, having missed an earlier train.

"Well, I hope to goodness she won't go and disturb Miss Beatty," grumbled Roger; and and then, half to himself, half to his companion, as the butler departed—"I don't believe she missed her train; she's one of the cool sort—does jolly well what she likes! I say, Colonel, do you like 'lady helps'? I don't!"

Half an hour later, Roger, having said good-night to his guest ten minutes before, was mounting the stairs on his own way to bed, when he heard in the distance the sound of a closing door and the rustle of a woman's dress.

Nurse Farmer, he supposed, who had been gossiping with Daphne. His face, as the candle shone upon it, expressed annoyance. Vaguely, he resented the kind of intimacy which had grown up lately between Daphne and her child's nurse. She was not the kind of person to make a friend of; she bullied Beatty; and she must be got rid of.

Yet when he entered his wife's room, everything was dark, and Daphne was apparently sound asleep. Her face was hidden from him; and he moved on tiptoe so as not to disturb her. Evidently it was not she who had been gossiping late. His mother, perhaps, with her maid.

CHAPTER VIII

In the course of that night Roger Barnes's fate was decided, while he lay, happily sleeping, beside his wife. Daphne, as soon as she heard his regular breathing, opened the eyes she had only pretended to close, and lay staring into the shadows of the room, in which a nightlight was burning. Presently she got up softly, put on a dressing-gown, and went to the fire, which she noiselessly replenished; drawing up a chair, she sank back into it, her arms folded. The strengthening firelight showed her small white face, amid the masses of her dark hair.

Her whole being was seething with passionate and revengeful thought. It was as though with violent straining and wrenching the familiar links and bulwarks of life were breaking down, and as if amid the wreck of them she found herself looking at goblin faces beyond, growing gradually used to them, ceasing to be startled by them, finding in them even a wild attraction and invitation.

"Her whole being was seething with passionate and revengeful thought."

So Roger had lied to her. Instead of a casual ride, involving a meeting with a few old acquaintances, as he had represented to her, he had been engaged that day in an assignation with Mrs. Fairmile, arranged beforehand, and carefully concealed from his wife. Miss Farmer had seen them coming out of a wood together hand in hand! In the public road, this!—not even so much respect for appearances as might have dictated the most elementary reticence and decency. The case was so clear that it sickened her; she shivered with cold and nausea as she lay there by the now glowing fire which yet gave her no physical comfort. Probably in the past their relation had gone much farther than Roger had ever confessed to his wife. Mrs. Fairmile was a woman who would stick at nothing. And if Daphne were not already betrayed, she could no longer protect herself. The issue was certain. Such women as Chloe Fairmile are not to be baulked of what they desire. Good women cannot fight them on equal terms. And as to any attempt to keep the affections of a husband who could behave in such a way to the wife who had given him her youth, herself, and all the resources and facilities of life, Daphne's whole being stiffened into mingled anguish and scorn as she renounced the contest. Knowing himself the traitor that he was, he could yet hold her, kiss her, murmur tender things to her, allow her to cry upon his breast, to stammer repentance and humbleness. Cowardly! False! Treacherous! She flung out her hands, rigid, before her in the darkness, as though for ever putting him away.

Anguish? Yes!—but not of such torturing quality as she could have felt a year, six months even, before this date. She was astonished that she could bear her life, that he could sit there in the night stillness, motionless, holding her breath even, while Roger slept there in the shadowed bed. Had this thing happened to her before their arrival at Heston, she must have fallen upon Roger in mad grief and passion, ready to kill him or herself; must at least have poured out torrents of useless words and tears. She could not have sat dumb like this; in misery, but quite able to think things out, to envisage all the dark possibilities of the future. And not only the future. By a perfectly logical diversion her thoughts presently went racing to the past. There was, so to speak, a suspension of the immediate crisis, while she listened to her own mind—while she watched her own years go by.

It was but rarely that Daphne let her mind run on her own origins. But on this winter night, as she sat motionless by the fire, she became conscious of a sudden detachment from her most recent self and life—a sudden violent turning against both—which naturally threw her back on the past, on some reflection upon what she had made of herself, by way of guide to what she might still make of herself, if she struck boldly, now, while there was yet time, for her own freedom and development.

As to her parents, she never confessed, even to herself, that she owed them anything, except, of course, the mere crude wealth that her father had left her. Otherwise she was vaguely ashamed of them both. And yet!—in her most vital qualities, her love of sensational effect, her scorn of half-measures, her quick, relentless imagination, her increasing ostentation and extravagance, she was the true child of the boastful mercurial Irishman who had married her Spanish mother as part of a trade bargain, on a chance visit to Buenos Ayres. For twenty years Daniel Floyd had leased and exploited, had ravaged and destroyed, great tracts of primæval forest in the northern regions of his adopted state, leaving behind him a ruined earth and an impoverished community, but building up the while a colossal fortune. He had learnt the arts of municipal "bossing" in one of the minor towns of Illinois, and had then migrated to Chicago, where for years he was the life and soul of all the bolder and more adventurous corruption of the city. A jovial, handsome fellow!—with an actor's face, a bright eye, and a slippery hand. Daphne had a vivid, and, on the whole, affectionate, remembrance of her father, of whom, however, she seldom spoke. The thought of her mother, on the other hand, was always unwelcome. It brought back recollections of storm and tempest; of wild laughter, and still wilder tears; of gorgeous dresses, small feet, and jewelled fingers.

No; her parents had but small place in that dramatic autobiography that Daphne was now constructing for herself. She was not their daughter in any but the physical sense; she was the daughter of her own works and efforts.

She leant forward to the fire, her face propped in her hands, going back in thought to her father's death, when she was fifteen; to her three years of cloying convent life, and her escape from it, as well as from the intriguing relations who would have kept her there; to the clever lawyer who had helped to put her in possession of her fortune, and the huge sums she had paid him for his services; to her search for education, her hungry determination to rise in the world, the friends she had made at college, in New York,

Philadelphia, Washington. She had been influenced by one *milieu* after another; she had worked hard, now at music, now at philosophy; had dabbled in girls' clubs, and gone to Socialist meetings, and had been all through driven on by the gadfly of an ever-increasing ambition.

Ambition for what! She looked back on this early life with a bitter contempt. What had it all come to? Marriage with Roger Barnes!—a hasty passion of which she was already ashamed, for a man who was already false to her.

What had made her marry him? She did not mince matters with herself in her reply. She had married him, influenced by a sudden, gust of physical inclination—by that glamour, too, under which she had seen him in Washington, a glamour of youth and novelty. If she had seen him first in his natural environment she would have been on her guard; she would have realized what it meant to marry a man who could help her own ideals and ambitions so little. And what, really, had their married life brought her? Had she ever been *sure* of Roger?—had she ever been able to feel proud of him, in the company of really distinguished men?—had she not been conscious, again and again, when in London, or Paris, or Berlin, that he was her inferior, that he spoiled her social and intellectual chances? And his tone toward women had always been a low one; no great harm in it, perhaps; but it had often wounded and disgusted her.

And then—for climax!—his concealment of the early love affair with Chloe Fairmile; his weakness and folly in letting her regain her hold upon him; his behaviour at the Brendon ball, the gossip which, as Agnes Farmer declared, was all over the neighbourhood, ending in the last baseness—the assignation, the lies, the hypocrisy of the afternoon!

Enough!—more than enough! What did she care what the English world thought of her? She would free and right herself in her own way, and they might hold up what hands they pleased. A passion of wounded vanity, of disappointed self-love swept through her. She had looked forward to the English country life; she had meant to play a great part in it. But three months had been enough to show her the kind of thing—the hopeless narrowness and Philistinism of these English back-waters. What did these small squires and country clergy know of the real world, the world that mattered to *her*, where people had free minds and progressive ideas? Her resentment of the *milieu* in which Roger expected her to live subtly swelled and strengthened her wrath against himself; it made the soil from which sprang a sudden growth of angry will—violent and destructive. There was in her little or none of that affinity with a traditional, a parent England, which is present in so many Americans, which emerges in them like buried land from the waters. On the contrary, the pressure of race and blood in her was not towards, but against; not friendly, but hostile. The nearer she came to the English life, the more certain forces in her, deeply infused, rose up and made their protest. The Celtic and Latin strains that were mingled in her, their natural sympathies and repulsions, which had been indistinct in the girl, overlaid by the deposits of the current American world, were becoming dominant in the woman.

Well, thank goodness, modern life is not as the old! There are ways out.

Midnight had just struck. The night was gusty, the north-west wind made fierce attacks on the square, comfortable house. Daphne rose slowly; she moved noiselessly across the floor; she stood with her arms behind her looking down at the sleeping Roger. Then a thought struck her; she reached out a hand to the new number of an American Quarterly which lay, with the paper knife in it, on a table beside the bed. She had ordered it in a mood of jealous annoyance because of a few pages of art criticism in it by Mrs. Fairmile, which impertinently professed to know more about the Vitali Signorelli than its present owner did; but she remembered also an article on "The Future for Women," which had seemed to her a fine, progressive thing. She turned the pages noiselessly—her eyes now on the unconscious Roger now on the book.

"All forms of contract—in business, education, religion, or law—suffer from the weakness and blindness of the persons making them—the marriage contract as much as any other. The dictates of humanity and common-sense alike show that the latter and most important contract should no more be perpetual than any of the others."

Again:—

"Any covenant between human beings that fails to produce or promote human happiness, cannot in the nature of things be of any force or authority; it is not only a right but a duty to abolish it."

And a little further:—

"Womanhood is the great fact of woman's life. Wifehood and motherhood are but incidental relations."

Daphne put down the book. In the dim light, the tension of her slender figure, her frowning brow, her locked arms and hands, made of her a threatening Fate hovering darkly above the man in his deep, defenceless sleep.

She was miserable, consumed with jealous anger. But the temptation of a new licence—a lawless law—was in her veins. Have women been trampled on, insulted, enslaved?—in America, at least, they may now stand on their feet. No need to cringe any more to the insolence and cruelty of men. A woman's life may be soiled and broken; but in the great human workshop of America it can be repaired. She remembered that in the majority of American divorces it is the woman who applies for relief. And why not? The average woman, when she marries, knows much less of life and the world than the average man. She is more likely—poor soul!—to make mistakes.

She drew closer to the bed. All round her glimmered the furniture and appointments of a costly room—the silver and tortoise-shell on the dressing-table, the long mirrors lining the farther wall, the silk hangings of the bed. Luxury, as light and soft as skill and money could make it—the room breathed it; and in the midst stood the young creature who had designed it, the will within her hardening rapidly to an irrevocable purpose.

Yes, she had made a mistake! But she would retrieve it. She would free herself. She would no longer put up with Roger, with his neglect and deceit—his disagreeable and ungrateful mother—his immoral friends—and this dull, soul-deadening English life.

Roger moved and murmured. She retreated a little, still looking at him fixedly. Was it the child's name? Perhaps. He dreamed interminably, and very often of Beatty. But it did not move her. Beatty, of course, was *her* child. Every child belongs to the mother in a far profounder sense than to the father. And he, too, would be free; he would naturally marry again.

Case after case of divorce ran through her mind as she stood there; the persons and circumstances all well known to her. Other stories also, not personally within her ken; the famous scandals of the time, much discussed throughout American society. Her wits cleared and steeled. She began to see the course that she must follow.

It would all depend upon the lawyers; and a good deal—she faced it—upon money. All sorts of technical phrases, vaguely remembered, ran through her mind. She would have to recover her American citizenship—she and the child. A domicile of six months in South Dakota, or in Wyoming—a year in Philadelphia—she began to recall information derived of old from Madeleine Verrier, who had, of course, been forced to consider all these things, and to weigh alternatives. Advice, of course, must be asked of her at once—and sympathy.

Suddenly, on her brooding, there broke a wave of excitement. Life, instead of being closed, as in a sense it is, for every married woman, was in a moment open and vague again; the doors flung wide to flaming heavens. An intoxication of recovered youth and freedom possessed her. The sleeping Roger represented things intolerable and outworn. Why should a woman of her gifts, of her opportunities, be chained for life to this commonplace man, now that her passion was over?—now that she knew him for what he was, weak, feather-brained, and vicious? She looked at him with a kind of exaltation, spurning him from her path.

But the immediate future!—the practical steps! What kind of evidence would she want?—what kind of witnesses? Something more, no doubt, of both than she had already. She must wait—temporize—do nothing rashly. If it was for Roger's good as well as her own that they should be free of each other—and she was fast persuading herself of this—she must, for both their sakes, manage the hateful operation without bungling.

What was the alternative? She seemed to ask it of Roger, as she stood looking down upon him. Patience?—with a man who could never sympathize with her intellectually or artistically?—the relations of married life with a husband who made assignations with an old love, under the eyes of the whole neighbourhood?—the narrowing, cramping influences of English provincial society? No! she was born for other and greater things, and she would grasp them. "My first duty is to myself—to my own development. We have absolutely no *right* to sacrifice ourselves—as women have been taught to do for thousands of years."

Bewildered by the rhetoric of her own thoughts, Daphne returned to her seat by the fire, and sat there wildly dreaming, till once more recalled to practical possibilities by the passage of the hours on the clock above her.

Miss Farmer? Everything, it seemed, depended on her. But Daphne had no doubts of her. Poor girl!—with her poverty-stricken home, her drunken father lately dismissed from his post, and her evident inclination towards this clever young fellow now employed in the house—Daphne rejoiced to think of what money could do, in this case at least; of the reward that should be waiting for the girl's devotion when the moment came; of the gifts already made, and the gratitude already evoked. No; she could be trusted; she had every reason to be true.

Some fitful sleep came to her at last in the morning hours. But when Roger awoke, she was half-way through her dressing; and when he first saw her, he noticed nothing except that she was paler than usual, and confessed to a broken night.

But as the day wore on it became plain to everybody at Heston—to Roger first and foremost—that something was much amiss. Daphne would not leave her sitting-room and her sofa; she complained of headache and over-fatigue; would have nothing to say to the men at work on the new decoration of the east wing of the house, who were clamouring for directions; and would admit nobody but Miss Farmer and her maid. Roger forced his way in once, only to be vanquished by the traditional weapons of weakness, pallor, and silence. Her face contracted and quivered as his step approached her; it was as though he trampled upon her; and he left her, awkwardly, on tiptoe, feeling himself as intrusively brutal as she clearly meant him to feel.

What on earth was the matter? Some new grievance against him, he supposed. After the softening, the quasi-reconciliation of the day before, his chagrin and disappointment were great. Impossible she should know anything of his ride with Chloe! There was not a soul in that wood; and the place was twenty miles from Heston. Again he felt the impulse to blurt it all out to her; but was simply repelled and intimidated by this porcupine mood in which she had wrapped herself. Better wait at least till she was a little more normal again. He went off disconsolately to a day's shooting.

Meanwhile, his own particular worry was sharp enough. Chloe had taken advantage of their casual *tête-à-tête*, as she had done before on several occasions, to claim something of the old relation, instead of accepting the new, like a decent woman; and in the face of the temptation offered him he had shown a weakness of which not only his conscience but his pride was ashamed. He realized perfectly that she had been trying during the whole autumn to recover her former hold on him, and he also saw clearly and bitterly that he was not strong enough to resist her, should he continue to be thrown with her; and not clever enough to baffle her, if her will were really set on recapturing him. He was afraid of her, and afraid of himself.

What, then, must he do? As he tramped about the wet fields and plantations with a keeper and a few beaters after some scattered pheasants, he was really, poor fellow! arguing out the riddle of his life. What would Herbert French advise him to do?—supposing he could put the question plainly to him, which of course was not possible. He meant honestly and sincerely to keep straight; to do his duty by Daphne and the child. But he was no plaster saint, and he could not afford to give Chloe Fairmile too many opportunities. To break at once, to carry off Daphne and leave Heston, at least for a time—that was the obviously prudent and reasonable course. But in her present mood it was of no use for him to propose it, tired as she seemed to be of Heston, and disappointed in the neighbours: any plan brought forward by him was doomed beforehand. Well then, let him go himself; he had been so unhappy during the preceding weeks it would be a jolly relief to turn his back on Heston for a time.

But as soon as he had taken his departure, Chloe perhaps would take hers; and if so, Daphne's jealousy would be worse than ever. Whatever deserts he might place between himself and Mrs. Fairmile, Daphne would imagine them together.

Meanwhile, there was that Lilliput bond, that small, chafing entanglement, which Chloe had flung round him in her persistence about the letters. There was, no doubt, a horrid scandal brewing about Mrs. Weightman, Chloe's old friend—a friend of his own, too, in former days. Through Chloe's unpardonable indiscretions he knew a great deal more about this lady's affairs than he had ever wished to know. And he well remembered the letter in question: a letter on which the political life or death of one of England's most famous men might easily turn, supposing it got out. But the letter was safe enough; not the least likely to come into dangerous hands, in spite of Chloe's absurd hypotheses. It was somewhere, no doubt, among the boxes in the locked room; and who could possibly get hold of it? At the same time he realized that as long as he had not found and returned it she would still have a certain claim upon him, a certain right to harass him with inquiries and confidential interviews, which, as a man of honour, he could not altogether deny.

A pheasant got up across a ploughed field where in the mild season the young corn was already green. Roger shot, and missed; the bird floated gaily down the wind, and the head keeper, in disgust, muttered bad language to the underling beside him.

But after that Barnes was twice as cheerful as before. He whistled as he walked; his shooting recovered; and by the time the dark fell, keepers and beaters were once more his friends.

The fact was that just as he missed the pheasant he had taken his resolution, and seen his way. He would have another determined hunt for that letter; he would also find and destroy his own letters to Chloe—those she had returned to him—which must certainly never fall into Daphne's hands; and then he would go away to London or the North, to some place whence he could write both to Chloe Fairmile and to his wife. Women like

Daphne were too quick; they could get out a dozen words to your one; but give a man time, and he could express himself. And, therewith, a great tenderness and compunction in this man's heart, and a steady determination to put things right. For was not Daphne Beatty's mother? and was he not in truth very fond of her, if only she would let him be?

Now then for the hunt. As he had never destroyed the letters, they must exist; but, in the name of mischief, where? He seemed to remember thrusting his own letters to Chloe into a desk of his schoolboy days which used to stand in his London sitting-room. Very likely some of hers might be there too. But the thought of his own had by now become a much greater anxiety to him than the wish to placate Chloe. For he was most uncomfortably aware that his correspondence with Chloe during their short engagement had been of a very different degree of fervour from that shown in the letters to Daphne under similar circumstances. As for the indelicacy and folly of leaving such documents to chance, he cursed it sorely.

How to look? He pondered it. He did not even know which attic it was that had been reserved at the time of the letting of Heston, and now held some of the old London furniture and papers. Well, he must manage it, "burgle" his own house, if necessary. What an absurd situation! Should he consult his mother? No; better not.

That evening General Hobson was expected for a couple of nights. On going up to dress for dinner, Roger discovered that he had been banished to a room on the farther side of the house, where his servant was now putting out his clothes. He turned very white, and went straight to his wife.

Daphne was on the sofa as before, and received him in silence.

"What's the meaning of this, Daphne?" The tone was quiet, but the breathing quick.

She looked at him—bracing herself.

"I must be alone! I had no sleep last night."

"You had neuralgia?"

"I don't know—I had no sleep. I must be alone."

His eyes and hers met.

"For to-night, then," he said briefly. "I don't know what's the matter with you, Daphne and I suppose it's no use to ask you. I thought, yesterday—but—however, there's no time to talk now. Are you coming down to dinner?"

"Not to dinner. I will come down for an hour afterwards."

He went away, and before he had reached his own room, and while the heat of his sudden passion still possessed him, it occurred to him that Daphne's behaviour might after all prove a godsend. That night he would make his search, with no risk of disturbing his wife.

The dinner in the newly decorated dining-room went heavily. Lady Barnes had grown of late more and more anxious and depressed. She had long ceased to assert herself in Daphne's presence, and one saw her as the British matron in adversity, buffeted by forces she did not understand; or as some minor despot snuffed out by a stronger.

The General, who had only arrived just in time to dress, inquired in astonishment for Daphne, and was told by Roger that his wife was not well, but would come down for a little while after dinner. In presence of the new splendours of Heston, the General had—in Roger's company—very little to say. He made the vague remark that the dining-room was "very fine," but he should not have known it again. Where was the portrait of Edward, and the full-length of Edward's father by Sir Francis Grant? Lady Barnes drew herself up, and said nothing. Roger hastily replied that he believed they were now in the passage leading to the billiard-room.

"What! that dark corner!" cried the General, looking with both distaste and hostility at the famous Signorelli—a full-length nude St. Sebastian, bound and pierced—which had replaced them on the dining-room wall. Who on earth ever saw such a picture in a dining-room? Roger must be a fool to allow it!

Afterwards the General and Lady Barnes wandered through the transformed house, in general agreement as to the ugliness and extravagance of almost everything that had been done, an agreement that was as balm to the harassed spirits of the lady.

"What have they spent?" asked the General, under his breath, as they returned to the drawing-room—"thousands and thousands, I should think! And there was no need for them to spend a penny. It is a sinful waste, and no one should waste money in these days—there are too many unemployed!" He drew up his spare person, with a terrier-like shake of the head and shoulders, as of one repudiating Mammon and all its works.

"Daphne has simply no idea of the value of money!" Lady Barnes complained, also under her breath. They were passing along one of the side corridors of the house, and there was no one in sight. But Roger's mother was evidently uneasy, as though Daphne might at any moment spring from the floor, or emerge from the walls. The General was really sorry for her.

"It's like all the rest of them—Americans, I mean," he declared; "they haven't our sense of responsibility. I saw plenty of that in the States."

Lady Barnes acquiesced. She was always soothed by the General's unfaltering views of British superiority.

They found Daphne in the drawing-room—a ghostly Daphne, in white, and covered with diamonds. She made a little perfunctory conversation with them, avoided all mention of the house, and presently, complaining again of headache, went back to her room after barely an hour downstairs.

The General whistled to himself, as he also retired to bed, after another and more private conversation with Lady Barnes, and half an hour's billiards with a very absent-minded host. By Jove, Laura wanted a change! He rejoiced that he was to escort her on the morrow to the London house of some cheerful and hospitable relations. Dollars, it seemed, were not everything, and he wished to heaven that Roger had been content to marry some plain English girl, with, say, a couple of thousand a year. Even the frugal General did not see how it could have been done on less. Roger no doubt had been a lazy, self-indulgent beggar. Yet he seemed a good deal steadier, and more sensible than he used to be; in spite of his wife, and the pouring out of dollars. And there was no doubt that he had grown perceptibly older. The General felt a vague pang of regret, so rare and so compelling had been the quality of Roger's early youth, measured at least by physical standards.

The house sank into sleep and silence. Roger, before saying good-night to his mother, had let fall a casual question as to the whereabouts of the room which still contained the *débris* of the London house. He must, he said, look up two or three things, some share certificates of his father's, for instance, that he had been in want of for some time. Lady Barnes directed him. At the end of the nursery wing, to the right. But in the morning one of the housemaids would show him. Had she the key? She produced it, thought no more of it, and went to bed.

He waited in his room till after midnight, then took off his shoes, his pride smarting, and emerged. There was one electric light burning in the hall below. This gave enough glimmer on the broad open landing for him to grope his way by, and he went noiselessly toward the staircase leading up to Beatty's rooms. Once, just as he reached it, he thought he caught the faint noise of low talking somewhere in the house, an indeterminate sound not to be located. But when he paused to listen, it had ceased and he supposed it to be only a windy murmur of the night.

He gained the nursery wing. So far, of course, the way was perfectly familiar. He rarely passed an evening without going to kiss Beatty in her cot. Outside the door of the night-nursery he waited a moment to listen. Was she snoozling among her blankets?—the darling! She still sucked her thumb, sometimes, poor baby, to send her to sleep, and it was another reason for discontent with Miss Farmer that she would make a misdemeanour of it. Really, that woman got on his nerves!

Beyond the nursery he had no knowledge whatever of his own house. The attics at Heston were large and rambling. He believed the servants were all in the other wing, but was not sure; he could only hope that he might not stumble on some handmaiden's room by mistake!

A door to the right, at the end of the passage. He tried the key. Thank goodness! It turned without too much noise, and he found himself on the threshold of a big lumber-room, his candle throwing lines of dusty light across it. He closed the door, set down the light, and looked round him in despair. The room was crowded with furniture, trunks, and boxes, in considerable confusion. It looked as though the men employed to move them had piled them there as they pleased; and Roger shrewdly suspected that his mother, from whom, in spite of her square and business-like appearance, his own indolence was inherited, had shrunk till now from the task of disturbing them.

He began to rummage a little. Papers belonging to his father—an endless series of them; some in tin boxes marked with the names of various companies, mining and other; some in leather cases, reminiscent of politics, and labelled "Parliamentary" or "Local Government Board." Trunks containing Court suits, yeomanry uniforms, and the like; a medley of old account books, photographs, worthless volumes, and broken ornaments: all the refuse that our too complex life piles about us was represented in the chaos of the room. Roger pulled and pushed as cautiously as he could, but making, inevitably, some noise in the process. At last! He caught sight of some belongings of his own and was soon joyfully detaching the old Eton desk, of which he was in search, from a pile of miscellaneous rubbish. In doing so, to his dismay, he upset a couple of old cardboard boxes filled with letters, and they fell with some clatter. He looked round instinctively at the door; but it was shut, and the house was well built, the walls and ceilings reasonably sound-proof. The desk was only latched—beastly carelessness, of course!—and inside it were three thick piles of letters, and a few loose ones below. His own letters to Chloe; and—by George!—the lost one!—among the others. He opened it eagerly, ran it through. Yes, the very thing! What luck! He laid it carefully aside a moment on a trunk near by, and sat with the other letters on his lap.

His fingers played with them. He almost determined to take them down unopened, and burn them, as they were, in his own room; but in the end he could not resist the temptation to look at them once more. He pulled off an india-rubber band from the latest packet, and was soon deep in them, at first half ashamed, half contemptuous. Calf love, of course! And he had been a precious fool to write such things. Then, presently, the headlong passion of them began to affect him, to set his pulses swinging. He fell to wondering at his own bygone facility, his own powers of expression. How did he ever write such a style! He, who could hardly get through a note now without blots and labour. Self-pity grew upon him, and self-admiration. By heaven! How could a woman treat a man—a man who could write to her like this—as Chloe had treated him!

The old smart revived; or rather, the old indelible impressions of it left on nerve and brain.

The letters lay on his knee. He sat brooding: his hands upon the packets, his head bowed. One might have thought him a man overcome and dissolved by the enervating memories of passion; but in truth, he was gradually and steadily reacting against them; resuming, and this time finally, as far as Chloe Fairmile was concerned, a man's mastery of himself. He thought of her unkindness and cruelty—of the misery he had suffered—and now of the reckless caprice with which, during the preceding weeks, she had tried to entangle him afresh, with no respect for his married life, for his own or Daphne's peace of mind.

He judged her, and therewith, himself. Looking back upon the four years since Chloe Fairmile had thrown him over, it seemed to him that, in some ways, he had made a good job of his life, and, in others, a bad one. As to the money, that was neither here nor there. It had been amusing to have so much of it; though of late Daphne's constant reminders that the fortune was hers and not his, had been like grit in the mouth. But he did not find that boundless wealth had made as much difference to him as he had expected. On the other hand, he had been much happier with Daphne than he had thought he should be, up to the time of their coming to Heston. She wasn't easy to live with, and she had been often, before now, ridiculously jealous; but you could not, apparently, live with a woman without getting very fond of her—he couldn't—especially if she had given you a child; and if Daphne had turned against him now, for a bit—well, he could not swear to himself that he had been free from blame; and it perhaps served him right for having gone out deliberately to the States to marry money—with a wife thrown in—in that shabby sort of way.

But, now, to straighten out this coil; to shake himself finally free of Chloe, and make Daphne happy again! He vowed to himself that he could and would make her happy—just as she had been in their early days together. The memory of her lying white and exhausted after child-birth, with the little dark head beside her, came across him, and melted him; he thought of her with longing and tenderness.

With a deep breath he raised himself on his seat; in the old Greek phrase, "the gods breathed courage into his soul"; and as he stretched out an indifferent hand toward Chloe's letters on the trunk, Roger Barnes had perhaps reached the highest point of his moral history; he had become conscious of himself as a moral being choosing good or evil; and he had chosen good. It was not so much that his conscience accused him greatly with regard to Chloe. For that his normal standards were not fine enough. It was rather a kind of "serious call," something akin to conversion, or that might have been conversion, which befell him in this dusty room, amid the night-silence.

As he took up Chloe's letters he did not notice that the door had quietly opened behind him, and that a figure stood on the threshold.

A voice struck into the stillness.

"Roger!"

He turned with a movement that scattered all his own letters on the floor. Daphne stood before him—but with the eyes of a mad woman. Her hand shook on the handle of the door.

"What are you doing here?" She flung out the question like a blow.

"Hallo, Daphne!—is that you?" He tried to laugh. "I'm only looking up some old papers; no joke, in all this rubbish." He pointed to it.

"What old papers?"

"Well, you needn't catechize me!" he said, nettled by her tone, "or not in that way, at any rate. I couldn't sleep, and I came up here to look for something I wanted. Why did you shut your door on me?"

He looked at her intently, his lips twitching a little. Daphne came nearer.

"It must be something you want very badly—something you don't want other people to see—something you're ashamed of!—or you wouldn't be searching for it at this time of night." She raised her eyes, still with the same strange yet flaming quiet, from the littered floor to his face. Then suddenly glancing again at the scattered papers—"That's your hand-writing!—they're your letters! letters to Mrs. Fairmile!"

"Well, and what do you make of that?" cried Roger, half wroth, half inclined to laugh. "If you want to know, they are the letters I wrote to Chloe Fairmile; and I, like a careless beast, never destroyed them, and they were stuffed away here. I have long meant to get at them and burn them, and as you turned me out to-night——"

"What is that letter in your hand?" exclaimed Daphne, interrupting him.

"Oh, that has nothing to do with you—or me——" he said, hastily making a movement to put it in his coat pocket. But in a second, Daphne, with a cry, had thrown herself upon him, to his intense amazement, wrestling with him, in a wild excitement. And as she did so, a thin woman, with frightened eyes, in a nurse's dress, came quickly into the room, as though Daphne's cry had signalled to her. She was behind Roger, and he was not aware of her approach.

"Daphne, don't be such a little fool!" he said indignantly, holding her off with one hand, determined not to give her the letter.

Then, all in a moment—without, as it seemed to him, any but the mildest defensive action on his part—Daphne stumbled and fell.

"Daphne!—I say!—--"

He was stooping over her in great distress to lift her up, when he felt himself vehemently put aside by a woman's hand.

"You ought to be ashamed of yourself, sir! Let me go to her."

He turned in bewilderment. "Miss Farmer! What on earth are you doing here?"

But in his astonishment he had given way to her, and he fell back pale and frowning, while, without replying, she lifted Daphne—who had a cut on her forehead and was half fainting—from the ground.

"Don't come near her, sir!" said the nurse, again warding him off. "You have done quite enough. Let me attend to her."

"You imagine that was my doing?" said Roger grimly. "Let me assure you it was nothing of the kind. And pray, were you listening at the door?"

Miss Farmer vouchsafed no reply. She was half leading, half supporting Daphne, who leant against her. As they neared the door, Roger, who had been standing dumb again, started forward.

"Let me take her," he said sternly. "Daphne!—send this woman away."

But Daphne only shuddered, and putting out a shaking hand, she waved him from her.

"You see in what a state she is!" cried Miss Farmer, with a withering look. "If you must speak to her, put it off, sir, at least till to-morrow."

Roger drew back. A strange sense of inexplicable disaster rushed upon him. He sombrely watched them pass through the door and disappear.

Daphne reached her own room. As the door closed upon them she turned to her companion, holding out the handkerchief stained with blood she had been pressing to her temple.

"You saw it all?" she said imperiously—"the whole thing?"

"All," said Miss Farmer. "It's a mercy you're not more hurt."

Daphne gave a hysterical laugh.

"It'll just do—I think it'll do! But you'll have to make a good deal out of it."

And sinking down by the fire, she burst into a passion of wild tears.

The nurse brought her sal volatile, and washed the small cut above her eyebrow.

"It was lucky we heard him," she said triumphantly. "I guessed at once he must be looking for something—I knew that room was full of papers."

A knock at the door startled them.

"Never mind." The nurse hurried across the room. "It's locked."

"How is my wife?" said Roger's strong, and as it seemed, threatening voice outside.

"She'll be all right, sir, I hope, if you'll leave her to rest. But I won't answer for the consequences if she's disturbed any more."

There was a pause, as though of hesitation. Then Roger's step receded.

Daphne pushed her hair back from her face, and sat staring into the fire. Everything was decided now. Yet she had rushed upstairs on Miss Farmer's information with no definite purpose. She only knew that—once again—Roger was hiding something from her—doing something secret and disgraceful—and she suddenly resolved to surprise and confront him. With a mind still vaguely running on the legal aspects of what she meant to do, she had bade the nurse follow her. The rest had been half spontaneous, half acting. It had struck her imagination midway how the incident could be turned—and used.

She was triumphant; but from sheer excitement she wept and sobbed through the greater part of the night.

PART III

CHAPTER IX

It was a cheerless February day, dark and slaty overhead, dusty below. In the East End streets paper and straw, children's curls, girls' pinafores and women's skirts were driven back and forward by a bitter wind; there was an ugly light on ugly houses, with none of that kind trickery of mist or smoke which can lend some grace on normal days even to Commercial Street, or to the network of lanes north of the Bethnal Green Road. The pitiless wind swept the streets—swept the children and the grown-ups out of them into the houses, or any available shelter; and in the dark and chilly emptiness of the side roads one might listen in fancy for the stealthy returning steps of spirits crueller than Cold, more tyrannous than Poverty, coming to seize upon their own.

In one of these side streets stood a house larger than its neighbours, in a bit of front garden, with some decrepit rust-bitten-railings between it and the road. It was an old dwelling overtaken by the flood of tenement houses, which spread north, south, east, and west of it. Its walls were no less grimy than its neighbours'; but its windows were outlined in cheerful white paint, firelight sparkled through its unshuttered panes, and a bright green door with a brass knocker completed its pleasant air. There were always children outside the Vicarage railings on winter evenings, held there by the spell of the green door and the firelight.

Inside the firelit room to the left of the front pathway, two men were standing—one of whom had just entered the house.

"My dear Penrose!—how very good of you to come. I know how frightfully busy you are."

The man addressed put down his hat and stick, and hastily smoothed back some tumbling black hair which interfered with spectacled eyes already hampered by short sight. He was a tall, lank, powerful fellow; anyone acquainted with the West-country would have known him for one of the swarthy, gray-eyed Cornish stock.

"I am pretty busy—but your tale, Herbert, was a startler. If I can help you—or Barnes—command me. He is coming this afternoon?"

Herbert French pointed his visitor to a chair.

"Of course. And another man—whom I met casually, in Pall Mall this morning—and had half an hour's talk with—an American naval officer—an old acquaintance of Elsie's—Captain Boyson—will join us also. I met him at Harvard before our wedding, and liked him. He has just come over with his sister for a short holiday, and I ran across him."

"Is there any particular point in his joining us?"

Herbert French expounded. Boyson had been an old acquaintance of Mrs. Roger Barnes before her marriage. He knew a good deal about the Barnes story—"feels, so I gathered, very strongly about it, and on the man's side; and when I told him that Roger had just arrived and was coming to take counsel with you and me this afternoon, he suddenly asked if he might come, too. I was rather taken aback. I told him that we were going, of course, to consider the case entirely from the English point of view. He still said, 'Let me come; I may be of use to you.' So I could only reply it must rest with Roger. They'll show him first into the dining-room."

Penrose nodded. "All right, as long as he doesn't mind his national toes trampled upon. So these are your new quarters, old fellow?"

His eyes travelled round the small book-lined room, with its shelves of poetry, history, and theology; its parish litter; its settle by the fire, on which lay a doll and a child's picture-book; back to the figure of the new vicar, who stood, pipe in hand, before the hearth, clad in a shabby serge suit, his collar alone betraying him. French's white hair showed even whiter than of old above the delicately blanched face; from his natural slenderness and smallness the East End and its life had by now stripped every superfluous ounce; yet, ethereal as his aspect was, not one element of the Meredithian trilogy— "flesh," "blood," or "spirit"—was lacking in it.

"Yes, we've settled in," he said quietly, as Penrose took stock.

"And you like it?"

"We do."

The phrase was brief; nor did it seem to be going to lead to anything more expansive. Penrose smiled.

"Well, now"—he bent forward, with a professional change of tone—"before he arrives, where precisely is this unhappy business? I gather, by the way, that Barnes has got practically all his legal advice from the other side, though the solicitors here have been coöperating?"

French nodded. "I am still rather vague myself. Roger only arrived from New York the day before yesterday. His uncle, General Hobson, died a few weeks ago, and Roger came rushing home, as I understand, to see if he could make any ready money out of his inheritance. Money, in fact, seems to be his chief thought."

"Money? What for? Mrs. Barnes's suit was surely settled long ago?"

"Oh, yes—months ago. She got her decree and the custody of the child in July."

"Remind me of the details. Barnes refused to plead?"

"Certainly. By the advice of the lawyers on both sides, he refused, as an Englishman, to acknowledge the jurisdiction of the Court."

"But he did what he could to stop the thing?"

"Of course. He rushed out after his wife as soon as he could trace where she had gone; and he made the most desperate attempts to alter her purpose. His letters, as far as I could make them out, were heart-rending. I very nearly went over to try and help him, but it was impossible to leave my work. Mrs. Barnes refused to see him. She was already at Sioux Falls, and had begun the residence necessary to bring her within the jurisdiction of the South Dakota Court. Roger, however, forced one or two interviews with her—most painful scenes!—but found her quite immovable. At the same time she was much annoyed and excited by the legal line that he was advised to take; and there was a moment when she tried to bribe him to accept the divorce and submit to the American court."

"To bribe him! With money?"

"No; with the child. Beatty at first was hidden away, and Roger could find no traces of her. But for a few weeks she was sent to stay with a Mrs. Verrier at Philadelphia, and Roger was allowed to see her, while Mrs. Barnes negotiated. It was a frightful dilemma! If he submitted, Mrs. Barnes promised that Beatty should go to him for two months every year; if not, and she obtained her decree, and the custody of the child, as she was quite confident of doing, he should never—as far as she could secure it—see Beatty again. He too, foresaw that she would win her suit. He was sorely tempted; but he stood firm. Then before he could make up his mind what to do as to the child, the suit came on, Mrs. Barnes got her decree, and the custody of the little girl."

"On the ground of 'cruelty,' I understand, and 'indignities'?"

French nodded. His thin cheek flushed.

"And by the help of evidence that any liar could supply!"

"Who were her witnesses?"

"Beatty's nurse—one Agnes Farmer—and a young fellow who had been employed on the decorative work at Heston. There were relations between these two, and Roger tells me they have married lately, on a partnership bought by Mrs. Barnes. While the work was going on at Heston the young man used to put up at an inn in the country town, and talk scandal at the bar."

"Then there was some local scandal—on the subject of Barnes and Mrs. Fairmile?"

"Possibly. Scandal *pour rire*! Not a soul believed that there was anything more in it than mischief on the woman's side, and a kind of incapacity for dealing with a woman as she deserved, on the man's. Mrs. Fairmile has been an *intrigante* from her cradle. Barnes was at one time deeply in love with her. His wife became jealous of her after the marriage, and threw them together, by way of getting at the truth, and he shilly-shallied with the situation, instead of putting a prompt end to it, as of course he ought to have done. He was honestly fond of his wife the whole time, and devoted to his home and his child."

"Well, she didn't plead, you say, anything more than 'cruelty' and 'indignities'. The scandal, such as it was, was no doubt part of the 'cruelty'?"

French assented.

"And you suspect that money played a great part in the whole transaction?"

"I don't *suspect*—the evidence goes a long way beyond that. Mrs. Barnes bought the show! I am told there are a thousand ways of doing it."

Penrose smoked and pondered.

"Well, then—what happened? I imagine that by this time Barnes had not much affection left for his wife?"

"I don't know," said French, hesitating. "I believe the whole thing was a great blow to him. He was never passionately in love with her, but he was very fond of her in his own way—increasingly fond of her—up to that miserable autumn at Heston. However, after the decree, his one thought was for Beatty. His whole soul has been wrapped up in that child from the first moment she was put into his arms. When he first realized that his wife meant to take her from him, Boyson tells me that he seemed to lose his head. He was like a person unnerved and bewildered, not knowing how to act or where to turn. First of all, he brought an action—a writ of *habeas corpus*, I think—to recover his daughter, as an English subject. But the fact was he had put it off too long——"

"Naturally," said Penrose, with a shrug. "Not much hope for him—after the decree."

"So he discovered, poor old fellow! The action was, of course, obstructed and delayed in every way, by the power of Mrs. Barnes's millions behind the scenes. His lawyers told him plainly from the beginning that he had precious little chance. And presently he found himself the object of a press campaign in some of the yellow papers—all of it paid for and engineered by his wife. He was held up as the brutal fortune-hunting Englishman, who had beguiled an American heiress to marry him, had carried her off to England to live upon her money, had then insulted her by scandalous flirtations with a lady to whom he had formerly been engaged, had shown her constant rudeness and unkindness, and had finally, in the course of a quarrel, knocked her down, inflicting shock and injury from which she had suffered ever since. Mrs. Barnes had happily freed herself from him, but he was now trying to bully her through the child—had, it was said, threatened to carry off the little girl by violence. Mrs. Barnes went in terror of him. America, however, would know how to protect both the mother and the child! You can imagine the kind of thing. Well, very soon Roger began to find himself a marked man in hotels, followed in the streets, persecuted by interviewers; and the stream of lies that found its way even into the respectable newspapers about him, his former life, his habits, etc., is simply incredible! Unfortunately, he gave some handle——"

French paused a moment.

"Ah!" said Penrose, "I have heard rumours."

French rose and began to pace the room.

"It is a matter I can hardly speak of calmly," he said at last. "The night after that first scene between them, the night of her fall—her pretended fall, so Roger told me—he went downstairs in his excitement and misery, and drank, one way and another, nearly a bottle of brandy, a thing he had never done in his life before. But——"

"He has often done it since?"

French raised his shoulders sadly, then added, with some emphasis. "Don't, however, suppose the thing worse than it is. Give him a gleam of hope and happiness, and he would soon shake it off."

"Well, what came of his action?"

"Nothing—so far. I believe he has ceased to take any interest in it. Another line of action altogether was suggested to him. About three months ago he made an attempt to kidnap the child, and was foiled. He got word that she had been taken to Charlestown, and he went there with a couple of private detectives. But Mrs. Barnes was on the alert, and when he discovered the villa in which the child had been living, she had been removed. It was a bitter shock and disappointment, and when he got back to New York in November, in the middle of an epidemic, he was struck down by influenza and pneumonia. It went pretty hard with him. You will be shocked by his appearance. Ecco! was there ever such a story! Do you remember, Penrose, what a magnificent creature he was that year he played for Oxford, and you and I watched his innings from the pavilion?"

There was a note of emotion in the tone which implied much. Penrose assented heartily, remarking, however, that it was a magnificence which seemed to have cost him dear, if, as no doubt was the case, it had won him his wife.

"But now, with regard to money; you say he wants money. But surely, at the time of the marriage, something was settled on him?"

"Certainly, a good deal. But from the moment she left him, and the Heston bills were paid, he has never touched a farthing of it, and never will."

"So that the General's death was opportune? Well, it's a deplorable affair! And I wish I saw any chance of being of use."

French looked up anxiously.

"Because you know," the speaker reluctantly continued, "there's nothing to be done. The thing's finished."

"Finished?" French's manner took fire. "And the law can do *nothing*! Society can do *nothing*, to help that man either to right himself, or to recover his child? Ah!"—he paused to listen—"here he is!"

A cab had drawn up outside. Through the lightly curtained windows the two within saw a man descend from it, pay the driver, and walk up the flagged passage leading to the front door.

French hurried to greet the new-comer.

"Come in, Roger! Here's George Penrose—as I promised you. Sit down, old man. They'll bring us some tea presently."

Roger Barnes looked round him for a moment without replying; then murmured something unintelligible, as he shook hands with Penrose, and took the chair which French pushed forward. French stood beside him with a furrowed brow.

"Well, here we are, Roger!—and if there's anything whatever in this horrible affair where an English lawyer can help you, Penrose is your man. You know, I expect, what a swell he is? A K. C. after seven years—lucky dog!—and last year he was engaged in an Anglo-American case not wholly unlike yours—Brown *v.* Brown. So I thought of him as the best person among your old friends and mine to come and give us some private informal help to-day, before you take any fresh steps—if you do take any."

"Awfully good of you both." The speaker, still wrapped in his fur coat, sat staring at the carpet, a hand on each of his knees. "Awfully good of you," he repeated vaguely.

Penrose observed the new-comer. In some ways Roger Barnes was handsomer than ever. His colour, the pink and white of his astonishing complexion, was miraculously vivid; his blue eyes were infinitely more arresting than of old; and the touch of physical weakness in his aspect, left evidently by severe illness, was not only not disfiguring, but a positive embellishment. He had been too ruddy in the old days, too hearty and splendid—a too obvious and supreme king of men—for our fastidious modern eyes. The grief and misfortune which had shorn some of his radiance had given a more human spell to what remained. At the same time the signs of change were by no means, all of them, easy to read, or reassuring to a friend's eye. Were they no more than physical and transient?

Penrose was just beginning on the questions which seemed to him important, when there was another ring at the front door. French got up nervously, with an anxious look at Barnes.

"Roger! I don't know whether you will allow it, but I met an American acquaintance of yours to-day, and, subject to your permission, I asked him to join our conference."

Roger raised his head—it might have been thought, angrily.

"Who on earth——?"

"Captain Boyson?"

The young man's face changed.

"I don't mind him," he said sombrely. "He's an awfully good sort. He was in Philadelphia a few months ago, when I was. He knows all about me. It was he and his sister who introduced me to—my wife."

French left the room for a moment, and returned accompanied by a fair-haired, straight-shouldered man, whom he introduced to Penrose as Captain Boyson.

Roger rose from his chair to shake hands.

"How do you do, Boyson? I've told them you know all about it." He dropped back heavily into his seat.

"I thought I might possibly put in a word," said the new-comer, glancing from Roger to his friends. "I trust I was not impertinent? But don't let me interrupt anything that was going on."

On a plea of chill, Boyson remained standing by the fire, warming his hands, looking down upon the other three. Penrose, who belonged to a military family, reminded himself, as he glanced at the American, of a recent distinguished book on Military Geography by a Captain Alfred Boyson. No doubt the same man. A capable face,—the face of the modern scientific soldier. It breathed alertness; but also some quality warmer and softer. If the general aspect had been shaped and moulded by an incessant travail of brain, the humanity of eye and mouth spoke dumbly to the humanity of others. The council gathered in the vicarage room felt itself strengthened.

Penrose resumed his questioning of Barnes, and the other two listened while the whole miserable story of the divorce, in its American aspects, unrolled. At first Roger showed a certain apathy and brevity; he might have been fulfilling a task in which he took but small interest; even the details of chicanery and corruption connected with the trial were told without heat; he said nothing bitter of his wife—avoided naming her, indeed, as much as possible.

But when the tale was done he threw back his head with sudden animation and looked at Boyson.

"Is that about the truth, Boyson? You know."

"Yes, I endorse it," said the American gravely. His face, thin and tanned, had flushed while Barnes was speaking.

"And you know what all their papers said of me—what *they* wished people to believe—that I wasn't fit to have charge of Beatty—that I should have done her harm?"

His eyes sparkled. He looked almost threateningly at the man whom he addressed. Boyson met his gaze quietly.

"I didn't believe it."

There was a pause. Then Roger sprang suddenly to his feet, confronting the men round him.

"Look here!" he said impatiently. "I want some money at once—and a good lot of it." He brought his fist down heavily on the mantelpiece. "There's this place of my uncle's, and I'm dashed if I can get a penny out of it! I went to his solicitors this morning. They drove me mad with their red-tape nonsense. It will take some time, they say, to get a mortgage on it, and meanwhile they don't seem inclined to advance me anything, or a hundred or two, perhaps. What's that? I lost my temper, and next time I go they'll turn me out, I dare say. But there's the truth. It's *money* I want, and if you can't help me to money it's no use talking."

"And when you get the money what'll you do with it?" asked Penrose.

"Pay half a dozen people who can be trusted to help me kidnap Beatty and smuggle her over the Canadian frontier. I bungled the thing once. I don't mean to bungle it again."

The answer was given slowly, without any bravado, but whatever energy of life there was in the speaker had gone into it.

"And there is no other way?" French's voice from the back was troubled.

"Ask him?" Roger pointed to Boyson.

"Is there any legal way, Boyson, in which I can recover the custody and companionship of my child?"

Boyson turned away.

"None that I know of—and I have made every possible inquiry."

"And yet," said Barnes, with emphasis, addressing the English barrister, "by the law of England I am still Daphne's husband and that child's legal guardian?"

"Certainly."

"And if I could once get her upon ground under the English flag, she would be mine again, and no power could take her from me?"

"Except the same private violence that you yourself propose to exercise."

"I'd take care of that!" said Roger briefly.

"How do you mean to do it?" asked French, with knit brows. To be sitting there in an English vicarage plotting violence against a woman disturbed him.

"He and I'll manage it," said the quiet voice of the American officer.

The others stared.

"*You?*" said French. "An officer in active service? It might injure your career!"

"I shall risk it."

A charming smile broke on Penrose's meditative face.

"My dear French, this is much more amusing than the law. But I don't quite see where *I* come in." He rose tentatively from his seat.

Boyson, however, did not smile. He looked from one to the other.

"My sister and I introduced Daphne Floyd to Barnes," he said steadily, "and it is my country, as I hold,—or a portion of it—that allows these villainies. Some day we shall get a great reaction in the States, and then the reforms that plenty of us are clamouring for will come about. Meanwhile, as of course you know"—he addressed French—"New Yorkers and Bostonians suffer almost as much from the abomination that Nevada and South Dakota call laws, as Barnes has suffered. Marriage in the Eastern States is as sacred as with you—South Carolina allows no divorce at all—but with this licence at our gates, no one is safe, and thousands of our women, in particular—for the women bring two-thirds of the actions—are going to the deuce, simply because they have the opportunity of going. And the children—it doesn't bear thinking of! Well—no good haranguing! I'm ashamed of my country in this matter—I have been for a long time—and I mean to help Barnes out, *coûte que coûte*! And as to the money, Barnes, you and I'll discuss that."

Barnes lifted a face that quivered, and he and Boyson exchanged looks.

Penrose glanced at the pair. That imaginative power, combined with the power of drudgery, which was in process of making a great lawyer out of a Balliol scholar, showed him something typical and dramatic in the two figures:—in Boyson, on the one hand, so lithe, serviceable, and resolved, a helpful, mercurial man, ashamed of his country in this one respect, because he adored her in so many others, penitent and patriot in one:—in Barnes, on the other, so heavy, inert, and bewildered, a ship-wrecked suppliant as it were, clinging to the knees of that very America which had so lightly and irresponsibly wronged him.

It was Penrose who broke the silence.

"Is there any chance of Mrs. Barnes's marrying again?" he asked.

Barnes turned to him.

"Not that I know of."

"There's no one else in the case?"

"I never heard of anyone." Roger gave a short, excited laugh. "What she's done, she's done because she was tired of me, not because she was in love with anyone else. That was her great score in the divorce case—that there was nobody."

Biting and twisting his lip, in a trick that recalled to French the beautiful Eton lad, cracking his brains in pupil-room over a bit of Latin prose, Roger glanced, frowning, from one to the other of these three men who felt for him, whose resentment of the wrong that had been done him, whose pity for his calamity showed plainly enough through their reticent speech.

His sense, indeed, of their sympathy began to move him, to break down his own self-command. No doubt, also, the fatal causes that ultimately ruined his will-power were already at work. At any rate, he broke out into sudden speech about his case. His complexion, now unhealthily delicate, like the complexion of a girl, had flushed deeply. As he spoke he looked mainly at French.

"There's lots of things you don't know," he said in a hesitating voice, as though appealing to his old friend. And rapidly he told the story of Daphne's flight from Heston. Evidently since his return home many details that were once obscure had become plain to him; and the three listeners could perceive how certain new information had goaded, and stung him afresh. He dwelt on the letters which had reached him during his first week's absence from home, after the quarrel—letters from Daphne and Miss Farmer, which were posted at intervals from Heston by their accomplice, the young architect, while the writers of them were hurrying across the Atlantic. The servants had been told that Mrs. Barnes, Miss Farmer, and the little girl were going to London for a day or two, and suspected nothing. "I wrote long letters—lots of them—to my wife. I thought I had made everything right—not that there ever had been anything wrong, you understand,—seriously. But in some ways I had behaved like a fool."

He threw himself back in his chair, pressing his hands on his eyes. The listeners sat or stood motionless.

"Well, I might have spared my pains. The letters were returned to me from the States. Daphne had arranged it all so cleverly that I was some time in tracing her. By the time I had got to Sioux Falls she was through a month of her necessary residence. My God!"—his voice dropped, became almost inaudible—"if I'd only carried Beatty off *then*!—then and there—the frontier wasn't far off—without waiting for anything more. But I wouldn't believe that Daphne could persist in such a monstrous thing, and, if she did, that any decent country would aid and abet her."

Boyson made a movement of protest, as though he could not listen any longer in silence.

"I am ashamed to remind you, Barnes,—again—that your case is no worse than that of scores of American citizens. We are the first to suffer from our own enormities."

"Perhaps," said Barnes absently, "perhaps."

His impulse of speech dropped. He sat, drearily staring into the fire, absorbed in recollection.

Penrose had gone. So had Boyson. Roger was sitting by the fire in the vicar's study, ministered to by Elsie French and her children. By common consent the dismal subject of the day had been put aside. There was an attempt to cheer and distract him. The little boy of four was on his knee, declaiming the "Owl and the Pussy Cat," while Roger submissively turned the pages and pointed to the pictures of that immortal history. The little girl of two, curled up on her mother's lap close by, listened sleepily, and Elsie, applauding and prompting as a properly regulated mother should, was all the time, in spirit, hovering pitifully about her guest and his plight. There was in her, as in Boyson, a touch of patriotic remorse; and all the pieties of her own being, all the sacred memories of her own life, combined to rouse in her indignation and sympathy for Herbert's poor friend. The thought of what Daphne Barnes had done was to her a monstrosity hardly to be named. She spoke to the young man kindly and shyly, as though she feared lest any chance word might wound him; she was the symbol, in her young motherliness, of all that Daphne had denied and forsaken. "When would America—dear, dear America!—see to it that such things were made impossible!"

Roger meanwhile was evidently cheered and braced. The thought of the interview to which Boyson had confidentially bidden him on the morrow ran warmly in his veins, and the children soothed him. The little boy especially, who was just Beatty's age, excited in him a number of practical curiosities. How about the last teeth? He actually inserted a coaxing and inquiring finger, the babe gravely suffering it. Any trouble with them? Beatty had once been very ill with hers, at Philadelphia, mostly caused, however, by some beastly, indigestible food that the nurse had let her have. And they allowed her to sit up much too late. Didn't Mrs. French think seven o'clock was late enough for any child not yet four? One couldn't say that Beatty was a very robust child, but healthy—oh yes, healthy!—none of your sickly, rickety little things.

The curtains had been closed. The street children, the electric light outside, were no longer visible. Roger had begun to talk of departure, the baby had fallen fast asleep in her mother's arms, when there was another loud ring at the front door.

French, who was expecting the headmaster of his church schools, gathered up some papers and left the room. His wife, startled by what seemed an exclamation from him in the hall outside, raised her head a moment to listen; but the sound of voices—surely a woman's voice?—died abruptly away, and the door of the dining-room closed. Roger heard nothing; he was laughing and crooning over the boy.

"The Pobble that lost his toes Had once as many as we."

The door opened. Herbert stood on the threshold beckoning to her. She rose in terror, the child in her arms, and went out to him. In a minute she reappeared in the doorway, her face ashen-white, and called to the little boy. He ran to her, and Roger rose, looking for the hat he had put down on entering.

Then French came in, and behind him a lady in black, dishevelled, bathed in tears. The vicar hung back. Roger turned in astonishment.

"Mother! You here? Mother!"—he hurried to her—"what's the matter?"

She tottered toward him with outstretched hands.

"Oh Roger, Roger!"

His name died away in a wail as she clasped him.

"What is it, mother?"

"It's Beatty—my son!—my darling Roger!" She put up her hands piteously, bending his head down to her. "It's a cable from Washington, from that woman, Mrs. Verrier. They did everything, Roger—it was only three days—and hopeless always. Yesterday convulsion came on—and this morning——" Her head dropped against her son's breast as her voice failed her. He put her roughly from him.

"What are you talking of, mother! Do you mean that Beatty has been ill?"

"She died last night. Roger—my darling son—my poor Roger!"

"Died—last night—Beatty?"

French in silence handed him the telegram. Roger disengaged himself and walked to the fireplace, standing motionless, with his back to them, for a minute, while they held their breaths. Then he began to grope again for his hat, without a word.

"Come home with me, Roger!" implored his mother, pursuing him. "We must bear it—bear it together. You see—she didn't suffer"—she pointed to the message—"the darling!—the darling!"

Her voice lost itself in tears. But Roger brushed her away, as though resenting her emotion, and made for the door.

French also put out a hand.

"Roger, dear, dear old fellow! Stay here with us—with your mother. Where are you going?"

Roger looked at his watch unsteadily.

"The office will be closed," he said to himself; "but I can put some things together."

"Where are you going, Roger?" cried Lady Barnes, pursuing him. Roger faced her.

"It's Tuesday. There'll be a White Star boat to-morrow."

"But, Roger, what can you do? She's gone, dear—she's gone. And before you can get there—long before—she will be in her grave."

A spasm passed over his face, into which the colour rushed. Without another word he wrenched himself from her, opened the front door, and ran out into the night.

CHAPTER X

"Was there ever anything so poetic, so suggestive?" said a charming voice. "One might make a new Turner out of it—if one just happened to be Turner!—to match 'Rain: Steam, and Speed.'"

"What would you call it—'Mist, Light, and Spring'?"

Captain Boyson leant forward, partly to watch the wonderful landscape effect through which the train was passing, partly because his young wife's profile, her pure cheek and soft hair, were so agreeably seen under the mingled light from outside.

They were returning from their wedding journey. Some six weeks before this date Boyson had married in Philadelphia a girl coming from one of the old Quaker stocks of that town, in whose tender steadfastness of character a man inclined both by nature and experience to expect little from life had found a happiness that amazed him.

The bridegroom, also, had just been appointed to the Military Attachéship at the Berlin Embassy, and the couple were, in fact, on their way south to New York and embarkation. But there were still a few days left of the honeymoon, of which they had spent the last half in Canada, and on this May night they were journeying from Toronto along the southern shore of Lake Ontario to the pleasant Canadian hotel which overlooks the pageant of Niagara. They had left Toronto in bright sunshine, but as they turned the corner of the lake westward, a white fog had come creeping over the land as the sunset fell.

But the daylight was still strong, the fog thin; so that it appeared rather as a veil of gold, amethyst, and opal, floating over the country, now parting altogether, now blotting out the orchards and the fields. And into the colour above melted the colour below. For the orchards that cover the Hamilton district of Ontario were in bloom, and the snow of the pear-trees, the flush of the peach-blossom broke everywhere through the warm cloud of pearly mist; while, just as Mrs. Boyson spoke, the train had come in sight of the long flashing line of the Welland Canal, which wound its way, outlined by huge electric lamps, through the sunset and the fog, till the lights died in that northern distance where stretched the invisible shore of the great lake. The glittering waterway, speaking of the labour and commerce of men, the blossom-laden earth, the white approaching mist, the softly falling night:—the girl-bride could not tear herself from the spectacle. She sat beside the window entranced. But her husband had captured her hand, and into the overflowing beauty of nature there stole the thrill of their love.

"All very well!" said Boyson presently. "But a fog at Niagara is no joke!"

The night stole on, and the cloud through which they journeyed grew denser. Up crept the fog, on stole the night. The lights of the canal faded, the orchards sank into darkness, and when the bride and bridegroom reached the station on the Canadian side the bride's pleasure had become dismay.

"Oh, Alfred, we shan't see anything!"

And, indeed, as their carriage made its slow progress along the road that skirts the gorge, they seemed to plunge deeper and deeper into the fog. A white darkness, as though of impenetrable yet glimmering cloud, above and around them; a white abyss beneath them; and issuing from it the thunderous voice of wild waters, dim first and distant, but growing steadily in volume and terror.

"There are the lights of the bridge!" cried Boyson, "and the towers of the aluminum works. But not a vestige of the Falls! Gone! Wiped out! I say, darling, this is going to be a disappointment."

Mrs. Boyson, however, was not so sure. The lovely "nocturne" of the evening plain had passed into a Vision or Masque of Force that captured the mind. High above the gulf rose the towers of the great works, transformed by the surging fog and darkness into some piled and castled fortress; a fortress of Science held by Intelligence. Lights were in the towers, as of genii at their work; lights glimmered here and there on the face of the farther cliff, as though to measure the vastness of the gorge and of that resounding vacancy towards which they moved. In front, the arch of the vast suspension bridge, pricked in light, crossed the gulf, from nothingness to nothingness, like that sky bridge on which the gods marched to Walhalla. Otherwise, no shape, no landmark; earth and heaven had disappeared.

"Here we are at the hotel," said Boyson. "There, my dear,"—he pointed ironically—"is the American Fall, and there—is the Canadian! Let me introduce you to Niagara!"

They jumped out of the carriage, and while their bags were being carried in they ran to the parapeted edge of the cliff in front of the hotel. Niagara thundered in their ears; the spray of it beat upon their faces; but of the two great Falls immediately in front of them they saw nothing whatever. The fog, now cold and clammy, enwrapped them; even the bright lights of the hotel, but a stone's throw distant, were barely visible; and the carriage still standing at the steps had vanished.

Suddenly, some common impulse born of the moment and the scene—of its inhuman ghostliness and grandeur—drew them to each other. Boyson threw his arm round his young wife and pressed her to him, kissing her face and hair, bedewed by the spray. She clung to him passionately, trembling a little, as the roar deafened them and the fog swept round them.

As the Boysons lingered in the central hall of the hotel, reading some letters which had been handed to them, a lady in black passed along the gallery overhead and paused a moment to look at the new arrivals brought by the evening train.

As she perceived Captain Boyson there was a quick, startled movement; she bent a moment over the staircase, as though to make sure of his identity, and then ran along the gallery to a room at the farther end. As she opened the door a damp cold air streamed upon her, and the thunder of the Falls, with which the hotel is perpetually filled, seemed to redouble.

Three large windows opposite to her were, in fact, wide open; the room, with its lights dimmed by fog, seemed hung above the abyss.

An invalid couch stood in front of the window, and upon it lay a pale, emaciated woman, breathing quickly and feebly. At the sound of the closing door, Madeleine Verrier turned.

"Oh, Daphne, I was afraid you had gone out! You do such wild things!"

Daphne Barnes came to the side of the couch.

"Darling, I only went to speak to your maid for a moment. Are you sure you can stand all this damp fog?"

As she spoke Daphne took up a fur cloak lying on a chair near, and wrapped herself warmly in it.

"I can't breathe when they shut the windows. But it is too cold for you."

"Oh, I'm all right in this." Daphne drew the cloak round her.

Inwardly she said to herself, "Shall I tell her the Boysons are here? Yes, I must. She is sure to hear it in some way."

So, stooping over the couch, she said:

"Do you know who arrived this evening? The Alfred Boysons. I saw them in the hall just now."

"They're on their honeymoon?" asked the faint voice, after a just perceptible pause.

Daphne assented. "She seems a pretty little thing."

Madeleine Verrier opened her tired eyes to look at Daphne. Mrs. Floyd—as Daphne now called herself—was dressed in deep black. The costly gown revealed a figure which had recently become substantial, and the face on which the electric light shone had nothing left in it of the girl, though Daphne Floyd was not yet thirty. The initial beauty of complexion was gone; so was the fleeting prettiness of youth. The eyes were as splendid as ever, but combined with the increased paleness of the cheeks, the greater prominence and determination of the mouth, and a certain austerity in the dressing of the hair, which was now firmly drawn back from the temples round which it used to curl, and worn high, *à la Marquise*, they expressed a personality—a formidable personality—in which self-will was no longer graceful, and power no longer magnetic. Madeleine Verrier gazed at her friend in silence. She was very grateful to Daphne, often very dependent on her. But there were moments when she shrank from her, when she would gladly never have seen her again. Daphne was still erect, self-confident, militant; whereas Madeleine knew herself vanquished—vanquished both in body and soul.

Certain inner miseries and discomforts had been set vibrating by the name of Captain Boyson.

"You won't want to see him or come across him?" she said abruptly.

"Who? Alfred Boyson? I am not afraid of him in the least. He may say what he pleases—or think what he pleases. It doesn't matter to me."

"When did you see him last?"

Daphne hesitated a moment. "When he came to ask me for certain things which had belonged to Beatty."

"For Roger? I remember. It must have been painful."

"Yes," said Daphne unwillingly, "it was. He was very unfriendly. He always has been—since it happened. But I bore him no malice"—the tone was firm—"and the interview was short."

"———" The half inaudible word fell like a sigh from Madeleine's lips as she closed her eyes again to shut out the light which teased them. And presently she added, "Do you ever hear anything now—from England?"

"Just what I might expect to hear—what more than justifies all that I did."

Daphne sat rigid on her chair, her hands crossed on her lap. Mrs. Verrier did not pursue the conversation.

Outside the fog grew thicker and darker. Even the lights on the bridge were now engulfed. Daphne began to shiver in her fur cloak. She put out a cold hand and took one of Mrs. Verrier's.

"Dear Madeleine! Indeed, indeed, you ought to let me move you from this place. Do let me! There's the house at Stockbridge all ready. And in July I could take you to Newport. I must be off next week, for I've promised to take the chair at a big meeting at Buffalo on the 29th. But I can't bear to leave you behind. We could make the journey quite easy for you. That new car of mine is very comfortable."

"I know it is. But, thank you, dear, I like this hotel; and it will be summer directly."

Daphne hesitated. A strong protest against "morbidness" was on her lips, but she did not speak it. In the mist-filled room even the bright fire, the electric lights, had grown strangely dim. Only the roar outside was real—terribly, threateningly real. Yet the sound was not so much fierce as lamentable; the voice of Nature mourning the eternal flow and conflict at the heart of things. Daphne knew well that, mingled with this primitive, cosmic voice, there was—for Madeleine Verrier—another; a plaintive, human cry, that was drawing the life out of her breast, the blood from her veins, like some baneful witchcraft of old. But she dared not speak of it; she and the doctor who attended Mrs. Verrier dared no longer name the patient's "obsession" even to each other. They had tried to combat it, to tear her from this place; with no other result, as it seemed, than to hasten the death-process which was upon her. Gently, but firmly, she had defied them, and they knew now that she would always defy them. For a year past, summer and winter, she had lived in this apartment facing the Falls; her nurses found her very patient under the incurable disease which had declared itself; Daphne came to stay with her when arduous engagements allowed, and Madeleine was always grateful and affectionate. But certain topics, and certain advocacies, had dropped out of their conversation—not by Daphne's will. There had been no spoken recantation; only the prophetess prophesied no more; and of late, especially when Daphne was not there—so Mrs. Floyd had discovered—a Roman Catholic priest had begun to visit Mrs. Verrier. Daphne, moreover, had recently noticed a small crucifix, hidden among the folds of the loose black dress which Madeleine commonly wore.

Daphne had changed her dress and dismissed her maid. Although it was May, a woodfire had been lighted in her room to counteract the chilly damp of the evening. She hung over it, loth to go back to the sitting-room, and plagued by a depression that not even her strong will could immediately shake off. She wished the Boysons had not come. She supposed that Alfred Boyson would hardly cut her; but she was tolerably certain that he would not wish his young wife to become acquainted with her. She scorned his disapproval of her; but she smarted under it. It combined with Madeleine's strange delusions to put her on the defensive; to call out all the fierceness of her pride; to make her feel herself the champion of a sound and reasonable view of life as against weakness and reaction.

Madeleine's dumb remorse was, indeed, the most paralyzing and baffling thing; nothing seemed to be of any avail against it, now that it had finally gained the upper hand. There had been dark times, no doubt, in the old days in Washington; times when the tragedy of her husband's death had overshadowed her. But in the intervals, what courage and boldness, what ardour in the declaration of that new Feminist gospel to which Daphne had in her own case borne witness! Daphne remembered well with what feverish readiness Madeleine had accepted her own pleas after her flight from England; how she had defended her against hostile criticism, had supported her during the divorce court proceedings, and triumphed in their result. "You are unhappy? And he deceived you? Well, then, what more do you want? Free yourself, my dear, free yourself! What right have you to bear more children to a man who is a liar and a shuffler? It is our generation that must suffer, for the liberty of those that come after!"

What had changed her? Was it simply the approach of mortal illness, the old questioning of "what dreams may come"? Superstition, in fact? As a girl she had been mystical and devout; so Daphne had heard.

Or was it the death of little Beatty, to whom she was much attached? She had seen something of Roger during that intermediate Philadelphia stage, when he and Beatty were allowed to meet at her house; and she had once or twice astonished and wounded Daphne at that time by sudden expressions of pity for him. It was she who had sent the cable message announcing the child's death, wording it as gently as possible, and had wept in sending it.

"As if I hadn't suffered too!" cried Daphne's angry thought. And she turned to look at the beautiful miniature of Beatty set in pearls that stood upon her dressing-table. There was something in the recollection of Madeleine's sensibility with regard to the child—as in that of her compassion for the father's suffering—that offended Daphne. It seemed a reflection upon herself, Beatty's mother, as lacking in softness and natural feeling.

On the contrary! She had suffered terribly; but she had thought it her duty to bear it with courage, not to let it interfere with the development of her life. And as for Roger, was it her fault that he had made it impossible for her to keep her promise? That she had been forced to separate Beatty from him? And if, as she understood now from various English correspondents, it was true that Roger had dropped out of decent society, did it not simply prove that she had guessed his character aright, and had only saved herself just in time?

It was as though the sudden presence of Captain Boyson under the same roof had raised up a shadowy adversary and accuser, with whom she must go on thus arguing, and hotly defending herself, in a growing excitement. Not that she would ever stoop to argue with Alfred Boyson face to face. How could he ever understand the ideals to which she had devoted her powers and her money since the break-up of her married life? He could merely estimate what she had done in the commonest, vulgarest way. Yet who could truthfully charge her with having obtained her divorce in order thereby to claim any fresh licence for herself? She looked back now with a cool amazement on that sudden rush of passion which had swept her into marriage, no less than the jealousy which had led her to break with Roger. She was still capable of many kinds of violence; but not, probably, of the violence of love. The influence of sex and sense upon her had weakened; the influence of ambition had increased. As in many women of Southern race, the period of hot blood had passed into a period of intrigue and domination. Her wealth gave her power, and for that power she lived.

Yes, she was personally desolate, but she had stood firm, and her reward lay in the fact that she had gathered round her an army of dependents and followers—women especially—to whom her money and her brains were indispensable. There on the table lay the plans for a new Women's College, on the broadest and most modern lines, to which she was soon to devote a large sum of money. The walls should have been up by now but for a quarrel with her secretary, who had become much too independent, and had had to be peremptorily dismissed at a moment's notice. But the plan was a noble one, approved by the highest authorities; and Daphne, looking to posterity, anticipated the recognition that she herself might never live to see. For the rest she had given herself—with reservations—to the Feminist movement. It was not in her nature to give herself wholly to anything; and she was instinctively critical of people who professed to be her leaders, and programmes to which she was expected to subscribe. Wholehearted devotion, which, as she rightly said, meant blind devotion, had never been her line; and she had been on one or two occasions offensively outspoken on the subject of certain leading persons in the movement. She was not, therefore, popular with her party, and did not care to be; her pride of money held her apart from the rank and file, the college girls, and typists, and journalists who filled the Feminist meetings, and often made themselves, in her eyes, supremely ridiculous, because of what she considered their silly provinciality and lack of knowledge of the world.

Yet, of course, she was a "Feminist"—and particularly associated with those persons in the suffrage camp who stood for broad views on marriage and divorce. She knew very well that many other persons in the same camp held different opinions; and in public or official gatherings was always nervously—most people thought arrogantly—on the lookout for affronts. Meanwhile, everywhere, or almost everywhere, her money gave her power, and her knowledge of it was always sweet to her. There was nothing in the world—no cause, no faith—that she could have accepted "as a little child." But everywhere, in her own opinion, she stood for Justice; justice for women as against the old primæval tyranny of men; justice, of course, to the workman, and justice to the rich. No foolish Socialism, and no encroaching Trusts! A lucid common sense, so it seemed to her, had been her cradle-gift.

And with regard to Art, how much she had been able to do! She had generously helped the public collections, and her own small gallery, at the house in Newport, was famous throughout England and America. That in the course of the preceding year she had found among the signatures, extracted from visitors by the custodian in charge, the name of Chloe Fairmile, had given her a peculiar satisfaction.

She walked proudly across the room, her head thrown back, every nerve tense. Let the ignorant and stupid blame her if they chose. She stood absolved. Memory reminded her, moreover, of a great number of kind and generous things—private things—that she had done with her money. If men like Herbert French, or Alfred Boyson, denounced her, there were many persons who felt warmly towards her—and had cause. As she thought of them the tears rose in her eyes. Of course she could never make such things public.

Outside the fog seemed to be lifting a little. There was a silvery light in the southeast, a gleam and radiance over the gorge. If the moon struggled through, it would be worth while slipping out after dinner to watch its play upon the great spectacle. She was careful to cherish in herself an openness to noble impressions and to the high poetry of nature and life. And she must not allow herself to be led by the casual neighbourhood of the Boysons into weak or unprofitable thought.

The Boysons dined at a table, gay with lights and flowers, that should have commanded the Falls but for the curtain of fog. Niagara, however, might flout them if it pleased; they could do without Niagara. They were delighted that the hotel, apparently, contained no one they knew. All they wanted was to be together, and alone. But the bride was tired by a long day in the train; her smiles began presently to flag, and by nine o'clock her husband had insisted on sending her to rest.

After escorting her upstairs Captain Boyson returned to the veranda, which was brightly lit up, in order to read some letters that were still unopened in his pocket. But before he began upon them he was seized once more by the wizardry of the scene. Was that indistinct glimmer in the far distance—that intenser white on white—the eternal cloud of spray that hangs over the Canadian Fall? If so, the fog was indeed yielding, and the full moon behind it would triumph before long. On the other hand, he could no longer see the lights of the bridge at all; the rolling vapour choked the gorge, and the waiter who brought him his coffee drily prophesied that there would not be much change under twenty-four hours.

He fell back upon his letters, well pleased to see that one among them came from Herbert French, with whom the American officer had maintained a warm friendship since the day of a certain consultation in French's East-End library. The letter was primarily one of congratulation, written with all French's charm and sympathy; but over the last pages of it Boyson's face darkened, for they contained a deplorable account of the man whom he and French had tried to save.

The concluding passage of the letter ran as follows:

"You will scarcely wonder after all this that we see him very seldom, and that he no longer gives us his confidence. Yet both Elsie and I feel that he cares for us as much as ever. And, indeed, poor fellow, he himself remains strangely lovable, in spite of what one must—alas!—believe as to his ways of life and the people with whom he associates. There is in him, always, something of what Meyers called 'the imperishable child.' That a man who might have been so easily led to good has been so fatally thrust into evil is one of the abiding sorrows of my life. How can I reproach him for his behaviour? As the law stands, he can never marry; he can never have legitimate children. Under the wrong he has suffered, and, no doubt, in consequence of that illness in New York, when he was badly nursed and cared for—from which, in fact, he has never wholly recovered—his will-power and nerve, which were never very strong, have given way; he broods upon the past perpetually, and on the loss of his child. Our poor Apollo, Boyson, will soon have lost himself wholly, and there is no one to help.

"Do you ever see or hear anything of that woman? Do you know what has become of her? I see you are to have a Conference on your Divorce Laws—that opinion and indignation are rising. For Heaven's sake, do something! I gather some appalling facts from a recent Washington report. One in twelve of all your marriages dissolved! A man or a woman divorced in one state, and still bound in another! The most trivial causes for the break-up of marriage, accepted and acted upon by corrupt courts, and reform blocked by a phalanx of corrupt interests! Is it all true? An American correspondent of mine—a lady—repeats to me what you once said, that it is the women who bring the majority of the actions. She impresses upon me also the remarkable fact that it is apparently only in a minority of cases that a woman, when she has got rid of her husband, marries someone else. It is not passion, therefore, that dictates many of these actions; no serious cause or feeling, indeed, of any kind; but rather an ever-spreading restlessness and levity, a readiness to tamper with the very foundations of society, for a whim, a nothing!—in the interests, of ten, of what women call their 'individuality'! No foolish talk here of being 'members one of another'! We have outgrown all that. The facilities are always there, and the temptation of them. 'The women—especially—who do these things,' she writes me, 'are moral anarchists. One can appeal to nothing; they acknowledge nothing.' Transformations infinitely far-reaching and profound are going on among us."

"'*Appeal to nothing!*' And this said of women, by a woman! It was of *men* that a Voice said long ago: 'Moses, because of the hardness of your hearts, suffered you to put away your wives'—on just such grounds apparently—trivial and cruel pretexts—as your American courts admit. 'But *I* say unto you!—*I say unto you!*'...

"Well, I am a Christian priest, incapable, of course, of an unbiassed opinion. My correspondent tries to explain the situation a little by pointing out that your women in America claim to be the superiors of your men, to be more intellectual, better-mannered, more refined. Marriage disappoints or disgusts them, and they impatiently put it aside. They break it up, and seem to pay no penalty. But you and I believe that they will pay it!—that there are divine avenging forces in the very law they tamper with—and that, as a nation, you must either retrace some of the steps taken, or sink in the scale of life.

"How I run on! And all because my heart is hot within me for the suffering of one man, and the hardness of one woman!"

Boyson raised his eyes. As he did so he saw dimly through the mist the figure of a lady, veiled, and wrapped in a fur cloak, crossing the farther end of the veranda. He half rose from his seat, with an exclamation. She ran down the steps leading to the road and disappeared in the fog.

Boyson stood looking after her, his mind in a whirl.

The manager of the hotel came hurriedly out of the same door by which Daphne Floyd had emerged, and spoke to a waiter on the veranda, pointing in the direction she had taken.

Boyson heard what was said, and came up. A short conversation passed between him and the manager. There was a moment's pause on Boyson's part; he still held French's letter in his hand. At last, thrusting it into his pocket, he hurried to the steps whereby Daphne had left the hotel, and pursued her into the cloud outside.

The fog was now rolling back from the gorge, upon the Falls, blotting out the transient gleams which had seemed to promise a lifting of the veil, leaving nothing around or beneath but the white and thunderous abyss.

CHAPTER XI

Daphne's purpose in quitting the hotel had been to find her way up the river by the road which runs along the gorge on the Canadian side, from the hotel to the Canadian Fall. Thick as the fog still was in the gorge she hoped to find some clearer air beyond it. She felt oppressed and stifled; and though she had told Madeleine that she was going out in search of effects and spectacle, it was in truth the neighbourhood of Alfred Boyson which had made her restless.

The road was lit at intervals by electric lamps, but after a time she found the passage of it not particularly easy. Some repairs to the tramway lines were going on higher up, and she narrowly escaped various pitfalls in the shape of trenches and holes in the roadway, very insufficiently marked by feeble lamps. But the stir in her blood drove her on; so did the strangeness of this white darkness, suffused with moonlight, yet in this immediate neighbourhood of the Falls, impenetrable. She was impatient to get through it; to breathe an unembarrassed air.

The roar at her left hand grew wilder. She had reached a point some distance from the hotel, close to the jutting corner, once open, now walled and protected, where the traveller approaches nearest to the edge of the Canadian Fall. She knew the spot well, and groping for the wall, she stood breathless and spray-beaten beside the gulf.

Only a few yards from her the vast sheet of water descended. She could see nothing of it, but the wind of its mighty plunge blew back her hair, and her mackintosh cloak was soon dripping with the spray. Once, far away, above the Falls, she seemed to perceive a few dim lights along the bend of the river; perhaps from one of the great power-houses that tame to man's service the spirits of the water. Otherwise—nothing! She was alone with the perpetual challenge and fascination of the Falls.

As she stood there she was seized by a tragic recollection. It was from this spot, so she believed, that Leopold Verrier had thrown himself over. The body had been carried down through the rapids, and recovered, terribly injured, in the deep eddying pool which the river makes below them. He had left no letter or message of any sort behind him. But the reasons for his suicide were clearly understood by a large public, whose main verdict upon it was the quiet "What else could he do?"

Here, then, on this very spot, he had stood before his leap. Daphne had heard him described by various spectators of the marriage. He had been, it seemed, a man of sensitive temperament, who should have been an artist and was a man of business; a considerable musician, and something of a poet; proud of his race and faith and himself irreproachable, yet perpetually wounded through his family, which bore a name of ill-repute in the New York business world; passionately grateful to his wife for having married him, delighting in her beauty and charm, and foolishly, abjectly eager to heap upon her and their child everything that wealth could buy.

"It was Madeleine's mother who made it hopeless," thought Daphne. "But for Mrs. Fanshaw—it might have lasted."

And memory called up Mrs. Fanshaw, the beautifully dressed woman of fifty, with her pride of wealth and family, belonging to the strictest sect of New York's social *élite*, with her hard, fastidious face, her formidable elegance and self-possession. How she had loathed the marriage! And with what a harpy-like eagerness had she seized on the first signs of Madeleine's discontent and *ennui*; persuaded her to come home; prepared the divorce; poisoned public opinion. It was from a last interview with Mrs. Fanshaw that Leopold Verrier had gone straight to his death. What was it that she had said to him?

Daphne lingered on the question; haunted, too, by other stray recollections of the dismal story—the doctor driving by in the early morning who had seen the fall; the discovery of the poor broken body; Madeleine's blanched stoicism, under the fierce coercion of her mother; and that strong, silent, slow-setting tide of public condemnation, which in this instance, at least, had avenged a cruel act.

But at this point Daphne ceased to think about her friend. She found herself suddenly engaged in a heated self-defence. What comparison could there be between her case and Madeleine's?

Fiercely she found herself going through the list of Roger's crimes; his idleness, treachery and deceit; his lack of any high ideals; his bad influence on the child; his luxurious self-indulgent habits, the lies he had told, the insults he had offered her. By now the story had grown to a lurid whole in her imagination, based on a few distorted facts, yet radically and monstrously untrue. Generally, however, when she dwelt upon it, it had power to soothe any smart of conscience, to harden any yearning of the heart, supposing she felt any. And by now she had almost ceased to feel any.

But to-night she was mysteriously shaken and agitated. As she clung to the wall, which alone separated her from the echoing gulf beyond, she could not prevent herself from thinking of Roger, Roger as he was when Alfred Boyson introduced him to her, when they first married, and she had been blissfully happy; happy in the possession of such a god-like creature, in the envy of other women, in the belief that he was growing more and more truly attached to her.

Her thoughts broke abruptly. "He married me for money!" cried the inward voice. Then she felt her cheeks tingling as she remembered her conversation with Madeleine on that very subject—how she had justified what she was now judging—how plainly she had understood and condoned it.

"That was my inexperience! Besides, I knew nothing then of Chloe Fairmile. If I had—I should never have done it."

She turned, startled. Steps seemed to be approaching her, of someone as yet invisible. Her nerves were all on edge, and she felt suddenly frightened. Strangers of all kinds visit and hang about Niagara; she was quite alone, known to be the rich Mrs. Floyd; if she were attacked—set upon——

The outline of a man's form emerged; she heard her name, or rather the name she had renounced.

"I saw you come in this direction, Mrs. Barnes. I knew the road was up in some places, and I thought in this fog you would allow me to warn you that walking was not very safe."

The voice was Captain Boyson's; and they were now plain to each other as they stood a couple of yards apart. The fog, however, was at last slightly breaking. There was a gleam over the nearer water; not merely the lights, but the span of the bridge had begun to appear.

Daphne composed herself with an effort.

"I am greatly obliged to you," she said in her most freezing manner. "But I found no difficulty at all in getting through, and the fog is lifting."

With a stiff inclination she turned in the direction of the hotel, but Captain Boyson stood in her way. She saw a face embarrassed yet resolved.

"Mrs. Barnes, may I speak to you a few minutes?"

Daphne gave a slight laugh.

"I don't see how I can prevent it. So you didn't follow me, Captain Boyson, out of mere regard for my personal safety?"

"If I hadn't come myself I should have sent someone," he replied quietly. "The hotel people were anxious. But I wished to come myself. I confess I had a very strong desire to speak to you."

"There seems to be nothing and no one to interfere with it," said Daphne, in a tone of sarcasm. "I should be glad, however, with your permission, to turn homeward. I see Mrs. Boyson is here. You are, I suppose, on your wedding journey?"

He moved out of her path, said a few conventional words, and they walked on. A light wind had risen and the fog was now breaking rapidly. As it gave way, the moonlight poured into the breaches that the wind made; the vast black-and-silver spectacle, the Falls, the gorge, the town opposite, the bridge, the clouds, began to appear in fragments, grandiose and fantastical.

Daphne, presently, seeing that Boyson was slow to speak, raised her eyebrows and attempted a remark on the scene. Boyson interrupted her hurriedly.

"I imagine, Mrs. Barnes, that what I wish to say will seem to you a piece of insolence. All the same, for the sake of our former friendship, I would ask you to bear with me."

"By all means!"

"I had no idea that you were in the hotel. About half an hour ago, on the veranda, I opened an English letter which arrived this evening. The news in it gave me great concern. Then I saw you appear, to my astonishment, in the distance. I asked the hotel manager if it were really you. He was about to send someone after you. An idea occurred to me. I saw my opportunity—and I pursued you."

"And here I am, at your mercy!" said Daphne, with sudden sharpness. "You have left me no choice. However, I am quite willing."

The voice was familiar yet strange. There was in it the indefinable hardening and ageing which seemed to Boyson to have affected the whole personality. What had happened to her? As he looked at her in the dim light there rushed upon them both the memory of those three weeks by the seaside years before, when he had fallen in love with her, and she had first trifled with, and then repulsed him.

"I wished to ask you a question, in the name of our old friendship; and because I have also become a friend—as you know—of your husband."

He felt, rather than saw, the start of anger in the woman beside him.

"Captain Boyson! I cannot defend myself, but I would ask you to recognize ordinary courtesies. I have now no husband."

"Of your husband," he repeated, without hesitation, yet gently. "By the law of England at least, which you accepted, and under which you became a British subject, you are still the wife of Roger Barnes, and he has done nothing whatever to forfeit his right to your wifely care. It is indeed of him and of his present state that I beg to be allowed to speak to you."

He heard a little laugh beside him—unsteady and hysterical.

"You beg for what you have already taken. I repeat, I am at your mercy. An American subject, Captain Boyson, knows nothing of the law of England. I have recovered my American citizenship, and the law of my country has freed me from a degrading and disastrous marriage!"

"While Roger remains bound? Incapable, at the age of thirty, of marrying again, unless he renounces his country—permanently debarred from home and children!"

His pulse ran quick. It was a strange adventure, this, to which he had committed himself!

"I have nothing to do with English law, nothing whatever! It is unjust, monstrous. But that was no reason why I, too, should suffer!"

"No reason for patience? No reason for pity?" said the man's voice, betraying emotion at last. "Mrs. Barnes, what do you know of Roger's present state?"

"I have no need to know anything."

"It matters nothing to you? Nothing to you that he has lost health, and character, and happiness, his child, his home, everything, owing to your action?"

"Captain Boyson!" she cried, her composure giving way, "this is intolerable, outrageous! It is humiliating that you should even expect me to argue with you. Yet," she bit her lip, angry with the agitation that would assail her, "for the sake of our friendship to which you appeal, I would rather not be angry. What you say is monstrous!" her voice shook. "In the first place, I freed myself from a man who married me for money."

"One moment! Do you forget that from the day you left him Roger has never touched a farthing of your money? That he returned everything to you?"

"I had nothing to do with that; it was his own folly."

"Yes, but it throws light upon his character. Would a mere fortune-hunter have done it? No, Mrs. Barnes!—that view of Roger does not really convince you, you do not really believe it."

She smiled bitterly.

"As it happens, in his letters to me after I left him, he amply confessed it."

"Because his wish was to make peace, to throw himself at your feet. He accused himself, more than was just. But you do not really think him mercenary and greedy, you *know* that he was neither! Mrs. Barnes, Roger is ill and lonely."

"His mode of life accounts for it."

"You mean that he has begun to drink, has fallen into bad company. That may be true. I cannot deny it. But consider. A man from whom everything is torn at one blow; a man of not very strong character, not accustomed to endure hardness.—Does it never occur to you that you took a frightful responsibility?"

"I protected myself—and my child."

He breathed deep.

"Or rather—did you murder a life—that God had given you in trust?"

He paused, and she paused also, as though held by the power of his will. They were passing along the public garden that borders the road; scents of lilac and fresh leaf floated over the damp grass; the moonlight was growing in strength, and the majesty of the gorge, the roar of the leaping water all seemed to enter into the moral and human scene, to accent and deepen it.

Daphne suddenly clung to a seat beside the path, dropped into it.

"Captain Boyson! I—I cannot bear this any longer."

"I will not reproach you any more," he said, quietly. "I beg your pardon. The past is irrevocable, but the present is here. The man who loved you, the father of your child, is alone, ill, poor, in danger of moral ruin, because of what you have done. I ask you to go to his aid. But first let me tell you exactly what I have just heard from England." He repeated the greater part of French's letter, so far as it concerned Roger.

"He has his mother," said Daphne, when he paused, speaking with evident physical difficulty.

"Lady Barnes I hear had a paralytic stroke two months ago. She is incapable of giving advice or help."

"Of course, I am sorry. But Herbert French——"

"No one but a wife could save him—no one!" he repeated with emphasis.

"I am *not* his wife!" she insisted faintly. "I released myself by American law. He is nothing to me." As she spoke she leant back against the seat and closed her eyes. Boyson saw clearly that excitement and anger had struck down her nervous power, that she might faint or go into hysterics. Yet a man of remarkable courtesy and pitifulness towards women was not thereby moved from his purpose. He had his chance; he could not relinquish it. Only there was something now in her attitude which recalled the young Daphne of years ago; which touched his heart.

He sat down beside her.

"Bear with me, Mrs. Barnes, for a few moments, while I put it as it appears to another mind. You became first jealous of Roger, for very small reason, then tired of him. Your marriage no longer satisfied you—you resolved to be quit of it; so you appealed to laws of which, as a nation, we are ashamed, which all that is best among us will, before long, rebel against and change. Our State system permits them—America suffers. In this case—forgive me if I put it once more as it appears to me—they have been used to strike at an Englishman who had absolutely no defence, no redress. And now you are free; he remains bound—so long, at least, as you form no other tie. Again I ask you, have you ever let yourself face what it means to a man of thirty to be cut off from lawful marriage and legitimate children? Mrs. Barnes! you know what a man is, his strength and his weakness. Are you really willing that Roger should sink into degradation in order that you may punish him for some offence to your pride or your feeling? It may be too late! He may, as French fears, have fallen into some fatal entanglement; it may not be possible to restore his health. He may not be able"—he hesitated, then brought the words out firmly—"to forgive you. Or again, French's anxieties about him may be unfounded. But for God's sake go to him! Once on English ground you are his wife again as though nothing had happened. For God's sake put every thing aside but the thought of the vow you once made to him! Go back! I implore you, go back! I promise you that no happiness you have ever felt will be equal to the happiness that step would bring you, if only you are permitted to save him."

Daphne was by now shaking from head to foot. The force of feeling which impelled him so mastered her that when he gravely took her hand she did not withdraw it. She had a strange sense of having at last discovered the true self of the quiet, efficient, unpretending man she had known for so long and cast so easily aside. There was shock and excitement in it, as there is in all trials of strength between a man and a woman. She tried to hate and despise him, but she could not achieve it. She longed to answer and crush him, but her mind was a blank, her tongue refused its office. Surprise, resentment, wounded feeling made a tumult and darkness through which she could not find her way.

She rose at last painfully from her seat.

"This conversation must end," she said brokenly. "Captain Boyson, I appeal to you as a gentleman, let me go on alone."

He looked at her sadly and stood aside. But as he saw her move uncertainly toward a portion of the road where various trenches and pits made walking difficult, he darted after her.

"Please!" he said peremptorily, "this bit is unsafe."

He drew her hand within his arm and guided her. As he did so he saw that she was crying; no doubt, as he rightly guessed, from shaken nerves and wounded pride; for it did not seem to him that she had yielded at all. But this time he felt distress and compunction.

"Forgive me!" he said, bending over her. "But think of what I have said—I beg of you! Be kind, be merciful!"

Marriage à la mode

She made various attempts to speak, and at last she said, "I bear you no malice. But you don't understand me, you never have."

He offered no reply. They had reached the courtyard of the hotel. Daphne withdrew her hand. When she reached the steps she preceded him without looking back, and was soon lost to sight.

Boyson shook his head, lit a cigar, and spent some time longer pacing up and down the veranda. When he went to his wife's room he found her asleep, a vision of soft youth and charm. He stood a few moments looking down upon her, wondering in himself at what he had done. Yet he knew very well that it was the stirring and deepening of his whole being produced by love that had impelled him to do it.

Next morning he told his wife.

"Do you suppose I produced *any* effect?" he asked her anxiously. "If she really thinks over what I said, she *must* be touched! unless she's made of flint. I said all the wrong things—but I *did* rub it in."

"I'm sure you did," said his wife, smiling. Then she looked at him with a critical tenderness.

"You dear optimist!" she cried, and slipped her hand into his.

"That means you think I behaved like a fool, and that my appeal won't move her in the least?"

The face beside him saddened.

"Dear, dear optimist!" she repeated, and pressed his hand. He urged an explanation of her epithet. But she only said, thoughtfully:

"You took a great responsibility!"

"Towards her?"

She shook her head.

"No—towards him!"

Meanwhile Daphne was watching beside a death-bed. On her return from her walk she had been met by the news of fresh and grave symptoms in Mrs. Verrier's case. A Boston doctor arrived the following morning. The mortal disease which had attacked her about a year before this date had entered, so he reported, on its last phase. He talked of a few days—possibly hours.

The Boysons departed, having left cards of inquiry and sympathy, of which Mrs. Floyd took no notice. Then for Daphne there followed a nightmare of waiting and pain. She loved Madeleine Verrier, as far as she was capable of love, and she jealously wished to be all in all to her in these last hours. She would have liked to feel that it was she who had carried her friend through them; who had nobly sustained her in the dolorous past. To have been able to feel this would have been as balm moreover to a piteously wounded self-love, to a smarting and bitter recollection, which would not let her rest.

But in these last days Madeleine escaped her altogether. A thin-faced priest arrived, the same who had been visiting the invalid at intervals for a month or two. Mrs. Verrier was received into the Roman Catholic Church; she made her first confession and communion; she saw her mother for a short, final interview, and her little girl; and the physical energy required for these acts exhausted her small store. Whenever Daphne entered her room Madeleine received her tenderly; but she could speak but little, and Daphne felt herself shut out and ignored. What she said or thought was no longer, it seemed, of any account. She resented and despised Madeleine's surrender to what she held to be a decaying superstition; and her haughty manner toward the mild Oratorian whom she met occasionally on the stairs, or in the corridor, expressed her disapproval. But it was impossible to argue with a dying woman. She suffered in silence.

As she sat beside the patient, in the hours of narcotic sleep, when she relieved one of the nurses, she went often through times of great bitterness. She could not forgive the attack Captain Boyson had made upon her; yet she could not forget it. It had so far roused her moral sense that it led her to a perpetual brooding over the past, a perpetual restatement of her own position. She was most troubled, often, by certain episodes in the past, of which, she supposed Alfred Boyson knew least; the corrupt use she had made of her money; the false witnesses she had paid for; the bribes she had given. At the time it had seemed to her all part of the campaign, in the day's work. She had found herself in a *milieu* that demoralized her; her mind had become like "the dyer's hand, subdued to what it worked in." Now, she found herself thinking in a sudden terror, "If Alfred Boyson knew so and so!" or, as she looked down on Madeleine's dying face, "Could I even tell Madeleine that?" And then would come the dreary thought, "I shall never tell her anything any more. She is lost to me—even before death."

She tried to avoid thinking of Roger; but the memory of the scene with Alfred Boyson did, in truth, bring him constantly before her. An inner debate began, from which she could not escape. She grew white and ill with it. If she could have rushed away from it, into the full stream of life, have thrown herself into meetings and discussion, have resumed her place as the admired and flattered head of a particular society, she could easily have crushed and silenced the thoughts which tormented her.

But she was held fast. She could not desert Madeleine Verrier in death; she could not wrench her own hand from this frail hand which clung to it; even though Madeleine had betrayed the common cause, had yielded at last to that moral and spiritual cowardice which—as all freethinkers know—has spoiled and clouded so many death-beds. Daphne—the skimmer of many books—remembered how Renan—*sain et sauf*—had sent a challenge to his own end, and defying the possible weakness of age and sickness, had demanded to be judged by the convictions of life, and not by the terrors of death. She tried to fortify her own mind by the recollection.

The first days of June broke radiantly over the great gorge and the woods which surround it. One morning, early, between four and five o'clock, Daphne came in, to find Madeleine awake and comparatively at ease. Yet the preceding twenty-four hours had been terrible, and her nurses knew that the end could not be far off.

The invalid had just asked that her couch might be drawn as near to the window as possible, and she lay looking towards the dawn, which rose in fresh and windless beauty over the town opposite and the white splendour of the Falls. The American Fall was still largely in shadow; but the light struck on the fresh green of Goat Island and leaped in tongues of fire along the edge of the Horseshoe, turning the rapids above it to flame and sending shafts into the vast tower of spray that holds the centre of the curve. Nature was all youth, glitter and delight; summer was rushing on the gorge; the mingling of wood and water was at its richest and noblest.

Madeleine turned her face towards the gorge, her wasted hands clasped on her breast. She beckoned Daphne with a smile, and Daphne knelt down beside her.

"The water!" said the whispering voice; "it was once so terrible. I am not afraid—now."

"No, darling. Why should you be?"

"I know now, I shall see him again."

Daphne was silent.

"I hoped it, but I couldn't be certain. That was so awful. Now—I am certain."

"Since you became a Catholic?"

She made a sign of assent.

"I couldn't be uncertain—I *couldn't*!" she added with fervour, looking strangely at Daphne. And Daphne understood that no voice less positive or self-confident than that of Catholicism, no religion less well provided with tangible rites and practices, could have lifted from the spirit the burden of that remorse which had yet killed the body.

A little later Madeleine drew her down again.

"I couldn't talk, Daphne—I was afraid; but I've written to you, just bit by bit, as I had strength. Oh, Daphne——!"

Then voice and strength failed her. Her eyes piteously followed her friend for a little, and then closed.

She lingered through the day; and at night when the June starlight was on the gorge, she passed away, with the voice of the Falls in her dying ears. A tragic beauty—"beauty born of murmuring sound—had passed into her face;" and that great plunge of many waters, which had been to her in life the symbol of anguish and guilt, had become in some mysterious way the comforter of her pain, the friend of her last sleep.

A letter was found for Daphne in the little box beside her bed.

It ran thus:

Daphne, Darling,—

"It was I who first taught you that we may follow our own lawless wills, and that marriage is something we may bend or break as we will. But, oh! it is not so. Marriage is mysterious and wonderful; it is the supreme test of men and women. If we wrong it, and despise it, we mutilate the divine in ourselves.

"Oh, Daphne! it is a small thing to say 'Forgive!' Yet it means the whole world.—

"And you can still say it to the living. It has been my anguish that I could only say it to the dead.... Daphne, good-bye! I have fought a long, long fight, but God is master—I bless—I adore——"

Daphne sat staring at the letter through a mist of unwilling tears. All its phrases, ideas, preconceptions, were unwelcome, unreal to her, though she knew they had been real to Madeleine.

Yet the compulsion of the dead was upon her, and of her scene with Boyson. What they asked of her—Madeleine and Alfred Boyson—was of course out of the question; the mere thought of that humiliating word "forgiveness" sent a tingle of passion through her. But was there no third course?—something which might prove to all the world how full of resource and generosity a woman may be?

She pondered through some sleepless hours; and at last she saw her way plain.

Within a week she had left New York for Europe.

CHAPTER XII

The ship on which Daphne travelled had covered about half her course. On a certain June evening Mrs. Floyd, walking up and down the promenade deck, found her attention divided between two groups of her fellow-travellers; one taking exercise on the same deck as herself; the other, a family party, on the steerage deck, on which many persons in the first class paused to look down with sympathy as they reached the dividing rail aft.

The group on the promenade deck consisted of a lady and gentleman, and a boy of seven. The elders walked rapidly; holding themselves stiffly erect, and showing no sign of acquaintance with anyone on board. The child dragged himself wearily along behind them, looking sometimes from side to side at the various people passing by, with eyes no less furtive than his mother's. She was a tall and handsome woman, with extravagantly marine clothes and much false hair. Her companion, a bulky and ill-favoured man, glanced superciliously at the ladies in the deck chairs, bestowing always a more attentive scrutiny than usual on a very pretty girl, who was lying reading midway down, with a white lace scarf draped round her beautiful hair and the harmonious oval of her face. Daphne, watching him, remembered that she had see him speaking to the girl—who was travelling alone—on one or two occasions. For the rest, they were a notorious couple. The woman had been twice divorced, after misdoings which had richly furnished the newspapers; the man belonged to a financial class with which reputable men of business associate no more than they are obliged. The ship left them severely alone; and they retaliated by a manner clearly meant to say that they didn't care a brass farthing for the ship.

The group on the steerage deck was of a very different kind. It was made up of a consumptive wife, a young husband and one or two children. The wife's malady, recently declared, had led to their being refused admission to the States. They had been turned back from the emigrant station on Ellis Island, and were now sadly returning to Liverpool. But the courage of the young and sweet-faced mother, the devotion of her Irish husband, the charm of her dark-eyed children, had roused much feeling in an idle ship, ready for emotion. There had been a collection for them among the passengers; a Liverpool shipowner, in the first class, had promised work to the young man on landing; the mother was to be sent to a sanatorium; the children cared for during her absence. The family made a kind of nucleus round which whatever humanity—or whatever imitation of it—there was on board might gather and crystallize. There were other mournful cases indeed to be studied on the steerage deck, but none in which misfortune was so attractive.

As she walked up and down, or sat in the tea room catching fragments of the conversation round her, Daphne was often secretly angered by the public opinion she perceived, favourable in the one case, hostile in the other. How ignorant and silly it was—this public opinion. As to herself, she was soon aware that a few people on board had identified her and communicated their knowledge to others. On the whole, she felt herself treated with deference. Her own version of her story was clearly accepted, at least by the majority; some showed her an unspoken but evident sympathy, while her wealth made her generally interesting. Yet there were two or three in whom she felt or fancied a more critical attitude; who looked at her coolly, and seemed to avoid her. Bostonian Pharisees, no doubt!—ignorant of all those great expansions of the female destiny that were going forward.

The fact was—she admitted it—that she was abnormally sensitive. These moral judgments, of different sorts, of which she was conscious, floating as it were in the life around her, which her mind isolated and magnified, found her smarting and sore, and would not let her be. Her irritable pride was touched at every turn; she hardly knew why. She was not to be judged by anybody; she was her own defender and her own judge. If she was no longer a symbolic and sympathetic figure—like that young mother among her children—she had her own claims. In the secrecy of the mind she fiercely set them out.

The days passed, however, and as she neared the English shores her resistance to a pursuing thought became fainter. It was, of course, Boyson's astonishing appeal to her that had let loose the Avenging Goddesses. She repelled them with scorn; yet all the same they hurtled round her. After all, she was no monster. She had done a monstrous thing in a sudden brutality of egotism; and a certain crude state of law and opinion had helped her to do it, had confused the moral values and falsified her conscience. But she was not yet brutalized. Moreover, do what she would, she was still in a world governed by law; a world at the heart of which broods a power austere and immutable; a power which man did not make, which, if he clash with it, grinds him to powder. Its manifestations in Daphne's case were slight, but enough. She was not happy, that certainly was clear. She did not suppose she ever would be happy again. Whatever it was—just, heroic, or the reverse—the action by which she had violently changed her life had not been a success, estimated by results. No other man had attracted her since she had cast Roger off; her youth seemed to be deserting her; she saw herself in the glass every morning with discontent, even a kind of terror; she had lost her child. And in these suspended hours of the voyage, when life floats between sky and sea, amid the infinity of weaves, all that she had been doing since the divorce, her public "causes" and triumphs, the adulations with which she had been surrounded, began to seem to her barren and futile. No, she was not happy; what she had done had not answered; and she knew it.

One night, a night of calm air and silvery sea, she hung over the ship's side, dreaming rather miserably. The ship, aglow with lights, alive with movement, with talk, laughter and music, glided on between the stars and the unfathomable depths of the mid-Atlantic. Nothing, to north and south, between her and the Poles; nothing but a few feet of iron and timber between her and the hungry gulfs in which the highest Alp would sink from sight. The floating palace, hung by Knowledge above Death, just out of Death's reach, suggested to her a number of melancholy thoughts and images. A touch of more than Arctic cold stole upon her, even through this loveliness of a summer night; she felt desperately unhappy and alone.

From the saloon came a sound of singing:

"An die Lippen wollt' ich pressen Deine kleine weisse Hand, Und mit Thränen sie benetzen Deine kleine weisse Hand."

The tears came to her eyes. She remembered that she, too, had once felt the surrender and the tenderness of love.

Then she brushed the tears away, angry with herself and determined to brood no more. But she looked round her in vain for a companion who might distract her. She had made no friends on board, and though she had brought with her a secretary and a maid, she kept them both at arm's length, and they never offered their society without an invitation.

What was she going to do? And why was she making this journey?

Because the injustice and absurdity of English law had distorted and besmirched her own perfectly legitimate action. They had given a handle to such harsh critics as Alfred Boyson. But she meant somehow to put herself right; and not only herself, but the great cause of woman's freedom and independence. No woman, in the better future that is coming, shall be forced either by law or opinion to continue the relations of marriage with a man she has come to despise. Marriage is merely proclaimed love; and if love fails, marriage has no further meaning or *raison d'être*; it comes, or should come, automatically to an end. This is the first article in the woman's charter, and without it marriage itself has neither value nor sanctity. She seemed to hear sentences of this sort, in her own voice, echoing about windy halls, producing waves of emotion on a sea of strained faces—women's faces, set and pale, like that of Madeleine Verrier. She had never actually made such a speech, but she felt she would like to have made it.

What was she going to do? No doubt Roger would resent her coming—would probably refuse to see her, as she had once refused to see him. Well, she must try and act with dignity and common sense; she must try and persuade him to recognize her good faith, and to get him to listen to what she proposed. She had her plan for Roger's reclamation, and was already in love with it. Naturally, she had never meant permanently to hurt or injure Roger! She had done it for his good as well as her own. Yet even as she put this plea forward in the inner tribunal of consciousness, she knew that it was false.

"You have murdered a life!" Well, that was what prejudiced and hide-bound persons like Alfred Boyson said, and no doubt always would say. She could not help it; but for her own dignity's sake, that moral dignity in which she liked to feel herself enwrapped, she would give as little excuse for it as possible.

Then, as she stood looking eastward, a strange thought struck her. Once on that farther shore and she would be Roger's wife again—an English subject, and Roger's wife. How ridiculous, and how intolerable! When shall we see some real comity of nations in these matters of international marriage and divorce?

She had consulted her lawyers in New York before starting; on Roger's situation first of all, but also on her own. Roger, it seemed, might take certain legal steps, once he was aware of her being again on English ground. But, of course, he would not take them. "It was never me he cared for—only Beatty!" she said to herself with a bitter perversity. Still the thought of returning within the range of the old obligations, the old life, affected her curiously. There were hours, especially at night, when she felt shut up with thoughts of Roger and Beatty—her husband and her child—just as of old.

How, in the name of justice, was she to blame for Roger's illness? Her irritable thoughts made a kind of grievance against him of the attack of pneumonia which she was told had injured his health. He must have neglected himself in some foolish way. The strongest men are the most reckless of themselves. In any case, how was it her fault?

One night she woke up suddenly, in the dawn, her heart beating tumultuously. She had been dreaming of her meeting—her possible meeting—with Roger. Her face was flushed, her memory confused. She could not recall the exact words or incidents of the dream, only that Roger had been in some way terrible and terrifying.

And as she sat up in her berth, trying to compose herself, she recalled the last time she had seen him at Philadelphia—a painful scene—and his last broken words to her, as he turned back from the door to speak them:—

"As to Beatty, I hold you responsible! She is my child, no less than yours. You shall answer to me! Remember that!"

Answer to him? Beatty was dead—in spite of all that love and science could do. Involuntarily she began to weep as she remembered the child's last days; the little choked cry, once or twice, for "Daddy!" followed, so long as life maintained its struggle, by a childish anger that he did not come. And then the silencing of the cry, and the last change and settling in the small face, so instinct already with feeling and character, so prophetic of the woman to be.

A grief, of course, never to be got over; but for which she, Daphne, deserved pity and tenderness, not reproaches. She hardened herself to meet the coming trial.

She arrived in London in the first week of July, and her first act was to post a letter to Herbert French, addressed to his East-End vicarage, a letter formally expressed and merely asking him to give the writer "twenty minutes' conversation on a subject of common interest to us both." The letter was signed "Daphne Floyd," and a stamped envelope addressed to "Mrs. Floyd" was enclosed. By return of post she received a letter from a person unknown to her, the curate, apparently, in charge of Mr. French's parish. The letter informed her that her own communication had not been forwarded, as Mr. French had gone away for a holiday after a threat of nervous breakdown in consequence of overwork; and business letters and interviews were being spared him as much as possible. "He is, however, much better, I am glad to say, and if the subject on which you wish to speak to him is really urgent, his present address is Prospect House, St. Damian's, Ventnor. But unless it is urgent it would be a kindness not to trouble him with it until he returns to town, which will not be for another fortnight."

Daphne walked restlessly up and down her hotel sitting-room. Of course the matter was urgent. The health of an East-End clergyman—already, it appeared, much amended—was not likely to seem of much importance to a woman of her temperament, when it stood in the way of her plans.

But she would not write, she would go. She had good reason to suppose that Herbert French would not welcome a visit from her; he might indeed very easily use his health as an excuse for not seeing her. But she must see him.

By mid-day she was already on her way to the Isle of Wight. About five o'clock she arrived at Ventnor, where she deposited maid and luggage. She then drove out alone to St. Damian's, a village a few miles north, through a radiant evening. The twinkling sea was alive with craft of all sizes, from the great liner leaving its trail of smoke along the horizon, to the white-sailed yachts close upon the land. The woods of the Undercliff sank softly to the blues and purple, the silver streaks and gorgeous shadows of the sea floor. The lights were broad and rich. After a hot day, coolness had come and the air was delightful.

But Daphne sat erect, noticing nothing but the relief of the lowered temperature after her hot and tiresome journey. She applied herself occasionally to natural beauty, as she applied herself to music or literature, but it is not to women of her type that the true passion of it—"the soul's bridegroom"—comes. And she was absorbed in thinking how she should open her business to Herbert French.

Prospect House turned out to be a detached villa standing in a garden, with a broad view of the Channel. Daphne sent her carriage back to the inn and climbed the steep drive which led up to the verandaed house. The front garden was empty, but voices—voices, it seemed, of children—came from behind the house where there was a grove of trees.

"Is Mr. Herbert French at home?" she asked of the maid who answered her bell.

The girl looked at her doubtfully.

"Yes, ma'am—but he doesn't see visitors yet. Shall I tell Mrs. French? She's in the garden with the children."

"No, thank you," said Daphne, firmly. "It's Mr. French I have come to see, and I am sure that he will wish to see me. Will you kindly give him my card? I will come in and wait."

And she brushed past the maid, who was intimidated by the visitor's fashionable dress and by the drooping feathers of her Paris hat, in which the sharp olive-skinned face with its magnificent eyes was picturesquely framed. The girl gave way unwillingly, showed Mrs. Floyd into a small study looking on the front garden, and left her.

"Elsie!" cried Herbert French, springing from the low chair in which he had been lounging in his shirt-sleeves with a book when the parlour-maid found him, "Elsie!"

His wife, who was at the other end of the lawn, playing with the children, the boy on her back and a pair of girl twins clinging to her skirts, turned in astonishment and hurried back to him.

"Mrs. Floyd?" They both looked at the card in bewilderment. "Who is it? Mrs. Floyd?"

Then French's face changed.

"What is this lady like?" he asked peremptorily of the parlour-maid.

"Well, sir, she's a dark lady, dressed very smart——"

"Has she very black eyes?"

"Oh yes, sir!"

"Young?"

The girl promptly replied in the negative, qualifying it a moment afterward by a perplexed "Well, I shouldn't say so, sir."

French thought a moment.

"Thank you. I will come in."

He turned to his wife with a rapid question, under his breath. "Where is Roger?"

Elsie stared at him, her colour paling.

"Herbert!—it can't—it can't——"

"I suspect it is—Mrs. Barnes," said French slowly. "Help me on with my coat, darling. Now then, what shall we do?"

"She can't have come to force herself on him!" cried his wife passionately.

"Probably she knows nothing of his being here. Did he go for a walk?"

"Yes, towards Sandown. But he will be back directly."

A quick shade of expression crossed French's face, which his wife knew to mean that whenever Roger was out by himself there was cause for anxiety. But the familiar trouble was immediately swallowed up in the new and pressing one.

"What can that woman have come to say?" he asked, half of himself, half of his wife, as he walked slowly back to the house. Elsie had conveyed the children to their nurse, and was beside him.

"Perhaps she repents!" The tone was dry and short; it flung a challenge to misdoing.

"I doubt it! But Roger?" French stood still, pondering. "Keep him, darling—intercept him if you can. If he must see her, I will come out. But we mustn't risk a shock."

They consulted a little in low voices. Then French went into the house and Elsie came back to her children. She stood thinking, her fine face, so open-browed and purely lined, frowning and distressed.

"You wished to see me, Mrs. Barnes?"

French had closed the door of the study behind him and stood without offering to shake hands with his visitor, coldly regarding her.

Daphne rose from her seat, reddening involuntarily.

"My name is no longer what you once knew it, Mr. French. I sent you my card."

French made a slight inclination and pointed to the chair from which she had risen.

"Pray sit down. May I know what has brought you here?"

Daphne resumed her seat, her small hands fidgeting on her parasol.

"I wished to come and consult with you, Mr. French. I had heard a distressing account of—of Roger, from a friend in America."

"I see," said French, on whom a sudden light dawned. "You met Boyson at Niagara—that I knew—and you are here because of what he said to you?"

"Yes, partly." The speaker looked round the room, biting her lip, and French observed her for a moment. He remembered the foreign vivacity and dash, the wilful grace of her youth, and marvelled at her stiffened, pretentious air, her loss of charm. Instinctively the saint in him knew from the mere look of her that she had been feeding herself on egotisms and falsehoods, and his heart hardened. Daphne resumed:

"If Captain Boyson has given you an account of our interview, Mr. French, it was probably a one-sided one. However, that is *not* the point. He *did* distress me very much by his account, which I gather came from you—of—of Roger, and although, of course, it is a very awkward matter for me to move in, I still felt impelled for old times' sake to come over and see whether I could not help you—and his other friends—and, of course, his mother——"

"His mother is out of the question," interrupted French. "She is, I am sorry to say, a helpless invalid."

"Is it really as bad as that? I hoped for better news. Then I apply to you—to you chiefly. Is there anything that I could do to assist you, or others, to——"

"To save him?" French put in the words as she hesitated.

Daphne was silent.

"What is your idea?" asked French, after a moment. "You heard, I presume, from Captain Boyson that my wife and I were extremely anxious about Roger's ways and habits; that we cannot induce him, or, at any rate, we have not yet been able to induce him, to give up drinking; that his health is extremely bad, and that we are sometimes afraid that there is now some secret in his life of which he is ashamed?"

"Yes," said Daphne, fidgeting with a book on the table. "Yes, that is what I heard."

"And you have come to suggest something?"

"Is there no way by which Roger can become as free as I now am!" she said suddenly, throwing back her head.

"By which Roger can obtain his divorce from you—and marry again? None, in English law."

"But there is—in Colonial law." She began to speak hurriedly and urgently. "If Roger were to go to New Zealand, or to Australia, he could, after a time, get a divorce for desertion. I know he could—I have inquired. It doesn't seem to be certain what effect my action—the American decree, I mean—would have in an English colony. My lawyers are going into it. But at any rate there is the desertion and then"—she grew more eager—"if he married abroad—in the Colony—the marriage would be valid. No one could say a word to him when he returned to England."

French looked at her in silence. She went on—with the unconscious manner of one accustomed to command her world, to be the oracle and guide of subordinates:—

"Could we not induce him to go? Could you not? Very likely he would refuse to see me; and, of course, he has, most unjustly to me, I think, refused to take any money from me. But the money might be provided without his knowing where it came from. A young doctor might be sent with him—some nice fellow who would keep him amused and look after him. At Heston he used to take a great interest in farming. He might take up land. I would pay anything—anything! He might suppose it came from some friend."

French smiled sadly. His eyes were on the ground. She bent forward.

"I beg of you, Mr. French, not to set yourself against me! Of course"—she drew herself up proudly—"I know what you must think of my action. Our views are different, irreconcilably different. You probably think all divorce wrong. We think, in America, that a marriage which has become a burden to either party is no marriage, and ought to cease. But that, of course"—she waved a rhetorical hand—"we cannot discuss. I do not propose for a moment to discuss it. You must allow me my national point of view. But surely we can, putting all that aside, combine to help Roger?"

"To marry again?" said French, slowly. "It can't, I fear, be done—what you propose—in the time. I doubt whether Roger has two years to live."

Daphne started.

"Roger!—to live?" she repeated, in horror. "What is really the matter? Surely nothing more than care and a voyage could set right?"

French shook his head.

"We have been anxious about him for some time. That terrible attack of septic pneumonia in New York, as we now know, left the heart injured and the lungs weakened. He was badly nursed, and his state of mind at the time—his misery and loneliness—left him little chance. Then the drinking habit, which he contracted during those wretched months in the States, has been of course sorely against him. However, we hoped against hope—Elsie and I—till a few weeks ago. Then someone, we don't know who, made him go to a specialist, and the verdict is—phthisis; not very advanced, but certain and definite. And the general outlook is not favourable."

Daphne had grown pale.

"We must send him away!" she said imperiously. "We must! A voyage, a good doctor, a dry climate, would save him, of course they would! Why, there is nothing necessarily fatal now in phthisis! Nothing! It is absurd to talk as though there were."

Again French looked at her in silence. But as she had lost colour, he had gained it. His face, which the East End had already stamped, had grown rosy, his eyes sparkled.

"Oh, do say something! Tell me what you suggest?" cried Daphne.

"Do you really wish me to tell you what I suggest?"

Daphne waited, her eyes first imploring, then beginning to shrink. He bent forward and touched her on the arm.

"Go, Mrs. Barnes, and ask your husband's forgiveness! What will come of it I do not know. But you, at least, will have done something to set yourself right—with God."

The Christian and the priest had spoken; the low voice in its intensity had seemed to ring through the quiet sun-flooded room. Daphne rose, trembling with resentment and antagonism.

"It is you, then, Mr. French, who make it impossible for me to discuss—to help. I shall have to see if I can find some other means of carrying out my purpose."

There was a voice outside. Daphne turned.

"Who is that?"

French ran to the glass door that opened on the veranda, and trying for an ordinary tone, waved somebody back who was approaching from without. Elsie came quickly round the corner of the house, calling to the new-comer.

But Daphne saw who it was and took her own course. She, too, went to the window, and, passing French, she stepped into the veranda.

"Roger!"

A man hurried through the dusk. There was an exclamation, a silence. By this time French was on the lawn, his wife's quivering hand in his. Daphne retreated slowly into the study and Roger Barnes followed her.

"Leave them alone," said French, and putting an arm round his wife he led her resolutely away, out of sound and sight.

Barnes stood silent, breathing heavily and leaning on the back of a chair. The western light from a side window struck full on him. But Daphne, the wave of excitement spent, was not looking at him. She had fallen upon a sofa, her face was in her hands.

"What do you want with me?" said Roger at last. Then, in a sudden heat, "By God, I never wished to see you again!"

Daphne's muffled voice came through her fingers.

"I know that. You needn't tell me so!"

Roger turned away.

"You'll admit it's an intrusion?" he said fiercely. "I don't see what you and I have got to do with each other now."

Daphne struggled for self-control. After all, she had always managed him in the old days. She would manage him now.

"Roger—I—I didn't come to discuss the past. That's done with. But—I heard things about you—that——"

"You didn't like?" he laughed. "I'm sorry, but I don't see what you have to do with them."

Daphne's hand fidgeted with her dress, her eyes still cast down.

"Couldn't we talk without bitterness? Just for ten minutes? It was from Captain Boyson that I heard——"

"Oh, Boyson, was that it? And he got his information from French—poor old Herbert. Well, it's quite true. I'm no longer fit for your—or his—or anybody's society."

He threw himself into an arm-chair, calmly took a cigarette out of a box that lay near, and lit it. Daphne at last ventured to look at him. The first and dominant impression was of something shrunken and diminished. His blue flannel suit hung loose on his shoulders and chest, his athlete's limbs. His features had been thinned and graved and scooped by fever and broken nights; all the noble line and proportion was still there, but for one who had known him of old the effect was no longer beautiful but ghastly. Daphne stared at him in dismay.

He on his side observed his visitor, but with a cooler curiosity. Like French he noticed the signs of change, the dying down of brilliance and of bloom. To go your own way, as Daphne had done, did not seem to conduce to a woman's good looks.

At last he threw in a dry interrogation.

"Well?"

"I came to try and help you," Daphne broke out, turning her head away, "to ask Mr. French what I could do. It made me unhappy——"

"Did it?" He laughed again. "I don't see why. Oh, you needn't trouble yourself. Elsie and Herbert are awfully good to me. They're all I want, or at any rate," he hesitated a moment, "they're all I *shall* want—from now on. Anyway, you know there'd be something grotesque in your trying your hand at reforming me."

"I didn't mean anything of the kind!" she protested, stung by his tone. "I—I wanted to suggest something practical—some way by which you might—release yourself from me—and also recover your health."

"Release myself from you?" he repeated. "That's easier said than done. Did you mean to send me to the Colonies—was that your idea?"

His smile was hard to bear. But she went on, choking, yet determined.

"That seems to be the only way—in English law. Why shouldn't you take it? The voyage, the new climate, would probably set you up again. You need only be away a short time."

He looked at her in silence a moment, fingering his cigarette.

"Thank you," he said at last, "thank you. And I suppose you offered us money? You told Herbert you would pay all expenses? Oh, don't be angry! I didn't mean anything uncivil. But," he raised himself with energy from his lounging position, "at the same time, perhaps you ought to know that I would sooner die a thousand times over than take a single silver sixpence that belonged to you!"

Their eyes met, his quite calm, hers sparkling with resentment and pain.

"Of course I can't argue with you if you meet me in that tone," she said passionately. "But I should have thought——"

"Besides," he interrupted her, "you say it is the only way. You are quite mistaken. It is not the only way. As far as freeing me goes, you could divorce me to-morrow—here—if you liked. I have been unfaithful to you. A strange way of putting it—at the present moment—between you and me! But that's how it would appear in the English courts. And as to the 'cruelty'—that wouldn't give *you* any trouble!"

Daphne had flushed deeply. It was only by a great effort that she maintained her composure. Her eyes avoided him.

"Mrs. Fairmile?" she said in a low voice.

He threw back his head with a sound of scorn.

"Mrs. Fairmile! You don't mean to tell me, Daphne, to my face, that you ever believed any of the lies—forgive the expression—that you, and your witnesses, and your lawyers told in the States—that you bribed those precious newspapers to tell?"

"Of course I believed it!" she said fiercely. "And as for lies, it was you who began them."

"You *believed* that I had betrayed you with Chloe Fairmile?" He raised himself again, fixing his strange deep-set gaze upon her.

"I never said——"

"No! To that length you didn't quite go. I admit it. You were able to get your way without it." He sank back in his chair again. "No, my remark had nothing to do with Chloe. I have never set eyes on her since I left you at Heston. But—there was a girl, a shop-girl, a poor little thing, rather pretty. I came across her about six months ago—it doesn't matter how. She loves me, she was awfully good to me, a regular little brick. Some day I shall tell Herbert all about her—not yet—though, of course, he suspects. She'd serve your purpose, if you thought it worth while. But you won't——"

"You're—living with her—now?"

"No. I broke with her a fortnight ago, after I'd seen those doctors. She made me see them, poor little soul. Then I went to say good-bye to her, and she," his voice shook a little, "she took it hard. But it's all right. I'm not going to risk her life, or saddle her with a dying man. She's with her sister. She'll get over it."

He turned his head towards the window, his eyes pursued the white sails on the darkening blue outside.

"It's been a bad business, but it wasn't altogether my fault. I saved her from someone else, and she saved me, once or twice, from blowing my brains out."

"What did the doctors say to you?" asked Daphne, brusquely, after a pause.

"They gave me about two years," he said, indifferently, turning to knock off the end of his cigarette. "That doesn't matter." Then, as his eyes caught her face, a sudden animation sprang into his. He drew his chair nearer to her and threw away his cigarette. "Look here, Daphne, don't let's waste time. We shall never see each other again, and there are a number of things I want to know. Tell me everything you can remember about Beatty that last six months—and about her illness, you understand—never mind repeating what you told Boyson, and he told me. But there's lots more, there must be. Did she ever ask for me? Boyson said you couldn't remember. But you must remember!"

He came closer still, his threatening eyes upon her. And as he did so, the dark presence of ruin and death, of things damning and irrevocable, which had been hovering over their conversation, approached with him—flapped their sombre wings in Daphne's face. She trembled all over.

"Yes," she said, faintly, "she did ask for you."

"Ah!" He gave a cry of delight. "Tell me—tell me at once—everything—from the beginning!"

And held by his will, she told him everything—all the piteous story of the child's last days—sobbing herself; and for the first time making much of the little one's signs of remembering her father, instead of minimizing and ignoring them, as she had done in the talk with Boyson. It was as though for the first time she were trying to stanch a wound instead of widening it.

He listened eagerly. The two heads—the father and mother—drew closer; one might have thought them lovers still, united by tender and sacred memories.

But at last Roger drew himself away. He rose to his feet.

"I'll forgive you much for that!" he said with a long breath. "Will you write it for me some day—all you've told me?"

She made a sign of assent.

"Well, now, you mustn't stay here any longer. I suppose you've got a carriage? And we mustn't meet again. There's no object in it. But I'll remember that you came."

She looked at him. In her nature the great deeps were breaking up. She saw him as she had seen him in her first youth. And, at last, what she had done was plain to her.

With a cry she threw herself on the floor beside him. She pressed his hand in hers.

"Roger, let me stay! Let me nurse you!" she panted. "I didn't understand. Let me be your friend! Let me help! I implore—I implore you!"

He hesitated a moment, then he lifted her to her feet decidedly, but not unkindly.

"What do you mean?" he said, slowly. "Do you mean that you wish us to be husband and wife again? You are, of course, my wife, in the eye of English law, at this moment."

"Let me try and help you!" she pleaded again, breaking into bitter tears. "I didn't—I didn't understand!"

He shook his head.

"You can't help me. I—I'm afraid I couldn't bear it. We mustn't meet. It—it's gone too deep."

He thrust his hands into his pockets and walked away to the window. She stood helplessly weeping.

When he returned he was quite composed again.

"Don't cry so," he said, calmly. "It's done. We can't help it. And don't make yourself too unhappy about me. I've had awful times. When I was ill in New York—it was like hell. The pain was devilish, and I wasn't used to being alone, and nobody caring a damn, and everybody believing me a cad and a bully. But I got over that. It was Beatty's death that hit me so hard, and that I wasn't there. It's that, somehow, I can't get over—that you did it—that you could have had the heart. It would always come between us. No, we're better apart. But I'll tell you something to comfort you. I've given up that girl, as I've told you, and I've given up drink. Herbert won't believe it, but he'll find it is so. And I don't mean to die before my time. I'm going out to Switzerland directly. I'll do all the correct things. You see, when a man *knows* he's going to die, well," he turned away, "he gets uncommonly curious as to what's going to come next."

He walked up and down a few turns. Daphne watched him.

"I'm not pious—I never was. But after all, the religious people profess to know something about it, and nobody else does. Just supposing it were true?"

He stopped short, looking at her. She understood perfectly that he had Beatty in his mind.

"Well, anyhow, I'm going to live decently for the rest of my time—and die decently. I'm not going to throw away chances. And don't trouble yourself about money. There's enough left to carry me through. Good-bye, Daphne!" He held out his hand to her.

She took it, still dumbly weeping. He looked at her with pity.

"Yes, I know, you didn't understand what you were doing. But you see, Daphne, marriage is——" he sought rather painfully for his words, "it's a big thing. If it doesn't make us, it ruins us; I didn't marry you for the best of reasons, but I was very fond of you—honour bright! I loved you in my way, I should have loved you more and more. I should have been a decent fellow if you'd stuck to me. I had all sorts of plans; you might have taught me anything. I was a fool about Chloe Fairmile, but there was nothing in it, you know there wasn't. And now it's all rooted up and done with. Women like to think such things can be mended, but they can't—they can't, indeed. It would be foolish to try."

Daphne sank upon a chair and buried her face in her hands. He drew a long and painful breath. "I'm afraid I must go," he said waveringly. "I—I can't stand this any longer. Good-bye, Daphne, good-bye."

She only sobbed, as though her life dissolved in grief. He drew near to her, and as she wept, hidden from him, he laid his hand a moment on her shoulder. Then he took up his hat.

"I'm going now," he said in a low voice. "I shan't come back till you have gone."

She heard him cross the room, his steps in the veranda. Outside, in the summer dark, a figure came to meet him. French drew Roger's arm into his, and the two walked away. The shadows of the wooded lane received them.

A woman came quickly into the room.

Elsie French looked down upon the sobbing Daphne, her own eyes full of tears, her hands clasped.

"Oh, you poor thing!" she said, under her breath. "You poor thing!" And she knelt down beside her and folded her arms round her.

So from the same heart that had felt a passionate pity for the victim, compassion flowed out on the transgressor. For where others feel the tragedy of suffering, the pure in heart realize with an infinitely sharper pain the tragedy of guilt.

THE END

CPSIA information can be obtained
at www.ICGtesting.com
Printed in the USA
LVHW050059120322
713252LV00009B/1292